GUN-PRODDY HOMBRE

BARRY CORD

SAGEBRUSH
Large Print Westerns

First published in Great Britain by Mills and Boon
First published in the United States by Arcadia House

First Isis Edition
published 2020
by arrangement with
Golden West Literary Agency

A catalogue record for this book is available
from the British Library.

ISBN 978–1–78541–848–8

Published by
Ulverscroft Limited
Anstey, Leicestershire

Set by Words & Graphics Ltd.
Anstey, Leicestershire
Printed and bound in Great Britain by
T. J. International Ltd., Padstow, Cornwall

This book is printed on acid-free paper

CHAPTER
ONE

He had been impatient to get here. Somehow he felt he owed it to Tony. He should have been here three months ago. And maybe if he had been, Tony would not now be dead.

Brett Havolin surveyed the log shack and the corral and barn. In the early morning light they looked ramshackle and dingy to his bleak gaze. He was not a cowman. The odor of stale manure, the empty corral, the rangeland running to the distant creek, held little meaning for him.

But this down-at-the-heels spread was his.

He thumbed his flat-crowned hat back on his head and slid out of the saddle. He was not used to riding, and his backside was sore and there was stiffness in his wide shoulders.

He had left Luke's Crossing, the rail town just over Warbonnet Pass, and ridden the better part of the night. Now he was here . . . but he saw nothing of Tony Mareno in this ramshackle spread Tony had boasted about.

A chesty rooster, most of its pinfeathers gone, strutted out from the barn and eyed him belligerently . . . A cat stalked into view from the corner of the corral. These two seemed to be the only living things on the Flying Club.

Brett Havolin's grin was cold. Even the name didn't fit Tony. Not "Two Drinks" Tony Mareno . . .

He went inside the house and found it cheerless and dingy; it depressed him. He stood in the middle of the big room with the smaller bedroom opening from it and surveyed the rusting cast-iron range, the stovepipe poking into the fieldstone chimney. There were signs that a family had once lived here . . . but not Tony. He had left no imprint Brett could recognize . . . and Brett had known Tony well.

He shook his head and took a cigar from his breast pocket and lighted it. It was a long way from Beaumont, he thought, this Texas valley — a long way to come to die . . .

The air felt suddenly close, and he walked out. He strolled over to the barn; the sun, less than two hours high, was already warm against the warped boards. He saw the feathers and scattered bones of half a dozen chickens, and thought of the field day it must have been for the coyotes . . . Somehow it seemed that this was what had happened to Tony when he came here.

He flung his cigar away and turned back to the sorrel and mounted. He had paid a hundred dollars for this animal and worn saddle back at Luke's Crossing; he knew they weren't worth it.

He swung away from the shack and headed for the main road some distance beyond, curling south, away from the line of the rocky creek. He rode slack and

2

brooding, knowing that there was no way he could make it up to Tony for having let him down . . .

Brett saw the rider on the rise ahead as he neared the wagon road . . . and caught the glint of sun from a rifle muzzle. He acted instinctively. He jerked the sorrel around and tried to get out of the saddle in a hurry.

The slug beat him. The sorrel reared and went over backward, and Brett took a nasty spill. He scraped his left hand and ploughed a furrow in the hard earth with his face.

It partially stunned him. When he recovered and scrambled to his feet he saw the rider had not moved. He dove behind the protection of his dead horse and cursed himself for having stowed his Colt in his saddle bag. Yet it would have done him little good at this distance. All of three hundred yards, he judged.

The sharpshooter on the rise had slid his rifle back into scabbard. Brett had a good look at him before the rider turned his chestnut away and disappeared over the rise . . .

Thirty minutes later, saddle heavy in his left hand, Brett paused by the side of the road to town and looked back. He had transferred his Colt to his waistband. He saw the wagon loom up and wiped his brow. The sun was already hot.

The farmer eyed him with suspicion as Brett stepped out into the road. "Ran into some trouble," Brett said. "I'd like a lift to Benton Wells —"

The farmer glanced at Brett's bruised face, at the saddle by the roadside. Lastly he noticed the Colt butt snugged against this man's hard belly. He nodded. "In back . . ."

Brett picked up his saddle, walked around to the tailgate, and hefted the kak over. He put both hands on the gate and vaulted into the bed . . . He sat on his saddle, his eyes hard.

The farmer glanced back at him, caught Brett's curt nod, and decided not to ask this man to sit on the seat beside him. He slapped his reins over the backs of the bays, and the wagon rolled . . .

All the way into town Brett Havolin sat on his saddle and nursed his smoldering anger in morose silence. It was a nine-mile ride from where he had thumbed a lift, and the morning coolness had given way to late summer heat, mixing dust and sweat on his blunt features.

He roused himself as the wagon wheels whirred through the dust of River Road. Benton Wells, he observed sourly, was a sizable cowtown sprawling along the south bluff of Taleback Creek.

From what Tony had written, which had been meager, Havolin had expected to find a raw frontier settlement. This town had a placid atmosphere of buggies and children and lazy afternoons. Even the women, he noted with cynically restrained appreciation, had the comfortable upholstered look one generally found in the bigger towns along the east bank of the Mississippi.

The main thoroughfare was wide and tree-shaded, dusty in the heat of late August. The wagon wheels churned up a fine spray behind them.

4

"This will do fine, right here," Brett finally said. The farmer hauled the bays in short and cast a close-mouthed look over his shoulder. Brett nodded briefly. "Thanks for the lift." He dropped his saddle over the tailgate and jumped down beside it and watched the man cluck his team on.

Havolin remained in the middle of the street, unmindful of the curious stares reaching out to him. He was a snub-nosed, square-jawed man in his late twenties, two inches shy of six feet. He had reddish hair which he wore cropped close, yet he let his sideburns grow midway down his jaw. He had made a bet with Tony to let them grow if he lost — and though Tony was now dead, Brett kept his end of the whimsical bargain.

The weathered, red-brick building across the street caught his eye, and he picked up his saddle and headed for it. Six-inch gilt lettering across the show window read: BANK OF GIBRALTAR. Brett dropped his saddle by the door and stepped inside.

The interior of the bank was cool and, except for the girl standing by the teller's cage, empty. Her voice was sharp in the drowsy quiet. "Now don't stand there and tell me that Walter didn't leave word for me —"

She turned with quick annoyance as Brett came in. She was a vivid, blue-eyed blonde, tall enough to look Brett in the eye, and wearing a summer gingham. At the moment there was a high, disturbed flush on her cheeks. And the backlash of her temper included Brett as she turned away from the sallow-faced man behind the grille.

5

"You'd look a lot better with your mouth closed!" she snapped as she walked past Brett. She had long legs and a spirited way of walking. Brett followed her out with his eyes and an appreciative grin. Then he walked to the teller's cage.

The man behind it wore a green eyeshade and a weary expression on his thin, sour face. He looked sharply at Brett, his eyes noting the dusty coat, the bruises, and started to shake his head. "It's about closing time, sir. Come back in the —"

Brett took a thick sheaf of bills from his coat and pushed them under the teller's nose. "I want to open an account," he said coldly. "I may change my mind in the morning."

The teller did a quick about-face. He bobbed his head several times. "I'm sure it can be arranged, Mr. — ?"

"Brett Havolin."

The teller riffled through the money. "Five thousand dollars," he counted. "That right, Mr. Havolin?"

Brett nodded. The man added respectfully: "I'll post it to your account, sir. And I'll have your book ready in a few minutes."

Brett said: "I'll wait." He turned around and leaned against the partition, staring idly through the show window. A man and a girl jogged by. The man was young, well set up and rode a chestnut horse. Brett caught the flash of white teeth against a sun-browned face as the rider smiled.

Havolin snapped: "I'll be right back!" to the teller. He was at the door in three long strides, flinging it open.

The riders were just turning in to the tie-rack in front of a three-decker, double-galleried structure that advertised itself as THE TRAIL HOUSE. Brett crossed the street at a fast walk, ducked beneath the short cross-pole under the nose of the chestnut and came up just as the man and the girl were mounting the hotel steps.

He murmured, "Pardon me, miss," as he nudged the girl aside, and as the tall man turned Brett sank his fist into the man's flat stomach, scraping his knuckles on the man's big brass buckle.

The tall youngster said: "Aw-w-w-w!" and Brett whipped a left hook across that snapped the other's head back sharply. An expensive soft gray Stetson skittered off curly brown hair, and the man, falling loosely, sprawled over it.

Brett rubbed his slightly bleeding knuckles into his palm, glanced at the open-mouthed girl, and politely touched his hat brim. "He had it coming," he explained curtly. "When he comes to, tell him I'll be seeing him again — with a bill. For one wall-eyed sorrel, worth to me one hundred dollars."

Color rushed back to the girl's face. She was dressed in faded blue Levis and a checked gingham blouse. Her face was lightly dusted with freckles, and these, along with a short, slightly uptilted nose, gave her a young and impudent look. Her eyes were gray, shot through with golden flecks — they were an angry gray now, dark as a stormy sky.

"You insolent, arrogant brute! Chet will — he'll kill you!"

"I won't lose any sleep over it." Brett grinned coldly. He nudged his hat brim again as he turned away, leaving her standing in spluttering, fuming rage on the hotel steps.

Brett strode jauntily back to the bank. He had not expected to run into the man who had so cold-bloodedly shot his horse from under him this morning — not as soon as he arrived in town. He still had no idea why the good-looking kid had killed his horse and then, with Brett at his mercy, had turned and ridden away. Nor did he know who he was.

But somehow this did not immediately interest Brett. The encounter on the hotel steps had taken the edge from his nursed anger. He felt in a better frame of mind as he reentered the bank.

The teller was just returning to the cage when Brett came up to the window. "Here's your book, Mr. Havolin." His tone held a barely restrained curiosity. "If the bank can be of any help — ?"

"It can," Brett said easily. "I'd like to get in touch with an attorney named Leo Kinsman."

The teller's eyes widened briefly. "Havolin — oh yes." He seemed suddenly embarrassed. "You're the man who inherited the Flying Club?"

Brett frowned. "What's so important about that?"

The teller swallowed. "Sorry. I meant no offense —"

"Leo Kinsman," Brett growled. "Where can I find him?"

"Mr. Kinsman has an office above the harness shop, two blocks south. But," the teller smiled knowingly, "I'd suggest that you try the Dusty Hole, a bar on Coyote Street, just around the next corner."

Brett said: "Thanks," and started to turn away.

"Where did you say you were staying in town, Mr. Havolin?" the teller asked hesitantly.

"I'm not staying in town at all," Brett answered shortly. "I'll be at the Flying Club after I conclude my business with Lawyer Kinsman."

The Dusty Hole evidently did a desultory business during the drowsy afternoon hours. Two men were teetering at the brass rail, arguing over the state of the nation in the loud, indignant tones safely used only between friends.

The man with his back to Brett wore a long black frock coat, and had muttonchop whiskers. His string tie had come undone and trailed down over the front of his soiled white shirt. A black beaver hat, long gone out of style, was pushed back on his high, shiny forehead. He had the puffy face and the red-veined nose of the habitual drinker, and he was shaking a finger into the face of the man facing him.

"I tell you free silver will put this country back on its feet! If I was among those knuckle-heads in Washington —"

The bartender, leaning on an elbow, looked as though he had heard this argument many times.

Brett walked up to the bar. "Lawyer Kinsman?"

The man in the black coat swung around.

"That's me, son."

"I want a word with you," Brett said.

Kinsman waved him off. "Get yourself a glass of beer, son. I'll be with you as soon as I set this jackass straight on some matters of national finance —"

"The name's Brett Havolin," Brett cut in sharply. "Tony Mareno was a friend of mine."

Kinsman's voice trailed. The dour-faced man glanced at Brett with sudden interest. Kinsman turned to Brett, his liquor-charged bluster evaporating. "Brett Havolin, eh?" He took the red-head by the arm and started for the door. "We'll talk in my office, son."

They left the Dusty Hole and turned right on River Road. Kinsman walked hurriedly, as though he didn't wish to be seen with this stranger to Benton Wells. Brett matched his stride, his lips thinning with cold amusement.

Kinsman's place of business was a long narrow room furnished with a dusty rolltop desk, an equally dusty bookcase holding a set of legal volumes which looked as though they were seldom used. The lawyer waved Brett to a stuffed chair and lowered himself into another by the desk. He began shuffling among an assortment of scattered papers and old envelopes on the desk and in the pigeonholes.

Suddenly he turned, frowning. "How do I know you're the man I wrote to?" he asked gruffly.

Brett reached inside his coat pocket and handed Kinsman a long envelope. Kinsman glanced at it, recognizing it as the one he had mailed two weeks before.

"I got a letter from Tony ten days before yours came," Brett said evenly. "I gathered from what he said that he was in good health. What did he die of?"

Kinsman leaned back, made a pyramid of his pudgy fingers. "The sheriff found Tony's body in Piute Creek, a hundred yards downstream from his cabin. It was wedged between rocks. His head was bashed in." The lawyer's reddish eyes met the frown in Brett's. He shrugged. "Both the sheriff and the coroner agreed it could have been an accident. There's white water for a stretch up there —"

Brett waited. Kinsman looked flustered. "You'd find out anyway," he muttered.

"Find out what?"

"There was a bullet in Tony, too. Two inches under his heart."

Brett said: "Ah!" softly. He took his eyes off Kinsman to stare at the blank wall. He was remembering six years of roughnecking up and down the oil fields of east Texas with Tony Mareno — hard-drinking, gambling, merrymaking years. Two young fellows with a lot of energy in them that needed outlet — two of a kind.

Why was it, he thought, that a man never really knew anyone else? Not even someone as close as Tony had been. What had there been in Tony that one night, in a dingy bar in Beaumont, that he could look Brett in the eye, a crooked grin on his lips, a lock of curly black hair down over one eye, and say quite seriously: "This is a devil of a life, Brett. I'm quitting. I'm going west, out where a man can breathe and think. I'll buy me a small spread, get married, raise some kids."

Brett put his calloused palm against Tony's jaw and shoved gently. "Go on, kid — get another drink. You're sobering up."

Tony had pushed his hand aside. "I'm serious, Brett. I'm pulling out of here in the morning."

Brett shook his head. "What about that lease you were coming in with me on?"

"Get hold of Sam Morrison, Brett. He's been wanting to come in with us —"

"You really mean it, Tony?" Brett's voice was surprised.

Tony grinned. "Only real idea I've had in years, Brett."

Havolin shook his head. "But you're not cut out for ranching, Tony. This is your game — oil. I'll give you six months, and you'll have a bellyful of that wide open country."

"Bet on it?" Tony had challenged.

"Sure. Even give you odds."

Tony waved his hand in front of Brett's face. "Not money. If I stay six months and am making a go of it, will you tear yourself away from Beaumont's bright lights and come out for a visit?"

Brett had taken the bet, confident that Tony would be back within six weeks. But it had been nine months since Tony had left, and he was the one who had welshed on his wager. Not welshed, really. He had intended to come.

But it had taken Kinsman's crisp, business-like note to bring him to this corner of Texas. The attorney had written: "Request that you come to Benton Wells immediately. You have been bequeathed certain properties known as the Flying Club by Mr. Tony

Mareno, recently deceased, and your presence here would expedite transfer of said properties . . ."

Brett brought his attention back to Kinsman. The lawyer was ruffling through some papers again. "There have been several offers to buy," he said matter-of-factly. "Three, in point of fact." He looked expectantly up at Brett.

"Who said the Flying Club was for sale?" Brett's tone was grim.

Kinsman shrugged. "Well, seeing as how you're a stranger to this part of the country, and —"

"Yes?"

Kinsman pulled his shoulders back in an effort to regain his dignity. "As your counsel in this matter, I would advise you to sell. All three offers have been more than fair. And if you'll allow me, Mr. Havolin, you don't look like the type of man who'll settle down on a two-by-four cattle ranch."

Brett's grin was crooked. "You'll be surprised at the type of man I can become," he said cheerfully. He tapped his index finger on the desk. "Where do I sign to take possession of the Flying Club?"

Kinsman's lips came together to make a harsh line. He pushed some papers toward the red-head. "Here — and here." He watched Brett sign with a flourish.

Havolin waited for the ink to dry, then picked up the papers and placed them in his inside coat pocket.

"Out of curiosity," he asked, easing back and sliding a cigar out of his breast pocket, "who made the offers?"

Kinsman shifted in his chair. "I should tell you to go to blazes," he said bluntly. "But —" he shrugged —

"one is Bully Armstrong — legal name is Frank. Owns the Big Diamond ranch west of town — his land runs clear to the Ridge. The other is Jack Thompson. Jack owns the Palace Bar, the Trail House, and hates Armstrong's guts." Kinsman wiped his lips with the back of his hand.

"The other?"

"Walter Baggett — president of the Bank of Gibraltar."

Brett nodded absently.

Kinsman made a tapping sound on his desk. "I should ride out with you to show you the place," he said. His tone indicated he wasn't eager.

"Don't bother. I got off the west-bound at Luke's Crossing last night, bought a cayuse and rode out to the ranch. Tony had written directions in one of his letters." Brett saw a look of slow surprise wash across Kinsman's face. "I didn't get a good look at the place," he added coldly. "A curly-headed character with a good eye shot the cayuse from under me. I thumbed a ride into town."

Kinsman settled back, a harsh grin sliding across his loose lips. "I still think you should sell, Havolin."

Brett got up, ignoring the man's advice. He was heading for the door when the lawyer's voice halted him. "That'll be two hundred dollars, Havolin!"

Brett turned. "For what?"

"Attorney's fee." Kinsman's jaw had a belligerent angle. "And if you've got any sense in that stubborn red head, you'll sell and clear out of this country, Havolin! Oil's your game, not cattle!"

14

Brett dug into a trouser pocket, peeled a hundred dollars from a shrunken roll, leaving about seventy dollars in small bills.

"Seeing as how I'm not taking your advice," he pointed out with dry humor, "we'll cut that fee in half." He tossed the hundred down on the desk, took a cigar from his breast pocket and added it to the money. "Your tip, Kinsman."

The lawyer picked up the cigar. He watched the redhead walk out. The glimpse of a walnut-handled Colt peeking almost coyly out of the parting of Brett's coat annoyed him.

"Damned cocky, aren't you?" he muttered belligerently. "You'll wish you had taken my advice, young feller, in less than a week." Brett's departure had roused courage in him, and he shook his fist at the door. "And danged if I won't be around to collect the other half of my fee when you get ready to leave, either!"

Heartened by his stand, and thirsty again, he picked up the five twenties, crumpled them carelessly inside his vest pocket.

Grabbing his beaver hat, he went out.

CHAPTER
TWO

Brett paused on the corner and lighted a cigar. The afternoon had changed during the time he had spent with Kinsman. There was a closeness in the air that was almost breathless. Glancing southward, he saw that dark clouds had piled up like puff balls on the horizon.

He scowled as he thought of the eleven-mile ride facing him before he would reach Tony's ranch — his ranch now.

He took a long pull on the cigar, his thoughts going back to the conversation he'd had with Tony's lawyer. Kinsman's grudging revelation that Tony had been shot to death puzzled him. The lawyer had seemed less concerned with this than with Brett's decision not to sell the Flying Club.

Havolin stood undecided, not relishing the thought of riding back to the lonely shack on which Tony had staked his future. He was used to people, to company, and he had a moment of wonder that Tony should have stuck it out as long as he had.

Brett had no intention of staying here. But Tony had been killed, and he knew he couldn't leave without finding out who had killed him. And why.

He let his restless glance move up the street and settle idly on the two riders jogging away from the Trail House. Recognition alerted him. His right hand lifted to hook his thumb into his belt, and he waited, a cold smile lengthening his lips.

The man he had hit and the girl who had been with him jogged up. Small puffs of dust kicked up behind them. They saw him. They jogged on past. The girl's eyes ran over him, cool and appraising, but without hostility. The youngster with her averted his gaze. His cheeks had a dark flush as he rode by.

Brett shrugged. The girl's partner had a build like the boys in the physical culture ads he had seen in the *Police Gazette*, but he evidently lacked a salting of guts.

He turned to head up River Road for the Trail House, and found himself looking into cornflower blue eyes he had seen before — at the teller's window in the Bank of Gibraltar. Only now these eyes held a lazy, provocative smile in their clear depths.

"Chet Armstrong's a big boy," the girl said. "But he's got a weak stomach. For a fight, that is."

Brett's lips curled in a brief smile. "He's right handy with a Winchester at three hundred yards," he recalled. His slow appraisal took in the rounded softness of this girl who would never see twenty again. His eyes came back to her face, and she caught the question in them.

"I'm Lorna Marlin. Your nearest neighbor."

"Oh?" He was genuinely surprised, and then the familiarity of her name brought Tony back to mind. This girl, he remembered, had often been mentioned in Tony's letters.

He smiled broadly. "I'm a poor hand at conversation on an empty stomach. If you'll name the place, I'll buy your dinner. My name's Brett Havolin," he added carelessly.

Lorna's smile brightened. "Polly's will give you a man-sized meal, home-cooked style. I'll have coffee with you."

The small restaurant was across the street from the Trail House. A clean and quiet place, it had red-checked tablecloths, and Polly did all the cooking herself. Brett looked across the table at the girl.

"I saw you hit Chet," she explained. Her tone was amused, lightly curious. "I had imagined you were a stranger to these parts, Mr. Havolin?"

"Am." He nodded. "Never been west of San Antonio until I came out here." His eyes met hers. "I was a friend of Tony Mareno's. You knew Tony?"

She made a small gesture with her shoulders. "Of course. Tony was a likable boy."

Brett settled back in his chair. He was thinking with cynical amusement that Tony was probably turning over in his grave at this remark. It had been a long time since any woman had called Tony a boy.

He waited until they were served before remarking seriously: "I'm glad you're taking a neighborly interest in me, Lorna. But I've got a hunch there's something more than friendly interest on your mind. You didn't stop me just to say, 'Hi, I'm your neighbor.'"

She dropped her eyes to her coffee, but not before Havolin glimpsed a sultry darkening of her glance, a shadowing that was like a gathering summer storm.

"You are a perceptive man, Mr. Havolin."

"Brett sounds better," he said. "Let's keep it neighborly."

"All right, Brett." She smiled. There was an impish gleam in her eyes now. "Call it a woman's curiosity. I did want to meet the man who, you might say, would be living next door to me." She made a small quick movement with her shapely shoulders. "I checked with Bob, the bank teller, and he told me who you were —"

"Is that all?"

"More curiosity," she admitted. "Who are you planning to sell the Flying Club to?"

He leaned back, a smile curving his lips. "Am I selling?"

"Aren't you?"

Stubbornness settled in him like an iron weight. This was the core of it, he was sure — this lay behind this girl's seeming friendliness. He felt both irritated and challenged.

"I've had offers," he acknowledged. "But I haven't decided."

She finished her coffee. "When you do, will you consider me?"

He was surprised, and showed it. "Why would you want to buy the Flying Club?"

Lorna's full red lips parted slightly, as though she were debating an inner question. "It could be because my mother and I like privacy," she said. "Does it really matter to you why I want to buy?"

He shrugged. "It might." He leaned across the table and caught her arm as she made a motion to rise. "Wait

— don't go yet." He was curious about this woman, and intrigued. He wanted to get inside her cool shell.

"Tony was your neighbor for close to nine months," he recalled. "Have you any idea who may have killed him?"

She arched her brows. "Was Tony killed? I thought he died of an accidental fall into Piute Creek."

Brett frowned. "A bullet isn't usually accidental," he growled.

She got up then, pulling on her gloves. "I see you've talked with Mr. Kinsman." She smiled, but now there was coolness in her manner. "You'll find that Benton Wells' legal light talks a great deal even for a lawyer, Mr. Havolin."

"Brett," he repeated stubbornly, watching her. He got to his feet and turned as he saw her glance lift past him and widen with amused expectancy.

A rangy man wearing a sheriff's star was threading his way among the diners, heading toward their table. He didn't look friendly.

Lorna was smiling as the lawman joined them, his eyes gliding quickly from her face and raking Brett with a hostile scowl. "This pilgrim annoying you, Miss Marlin?"

Brett looked him over coldly. The sheriff was a rangy man in his early forties, a good four inches taller than Brett. He had a broad, weather-beaten face in which pale gray eyes stood out sharply against the burnt coloring of his features. A long slab of a man, Brett judged — physically hard as a rock, but emotionally soft. Tied up inside when it came to dealing with a woman like Lorna.

The girl turned to the sheriff in the manner of a cat arching its back. "I wouldn't call it that, Ray," she purred. "But I think you can tell him what he wants to know. He's asking about Tony."

She was still smiling as she turned to Brett. "Remember me, Mr. Havolin, when you decide to sell the Flying Club. Please?" She moved around the table and quite deliberately brushed against the sheriff as she went past him. The lawman went red to the roots of his thinning brown hair.

Brett grinned. The sheriff's face hardened as he turned his attention to the redheaded stranger. "You get around *muy pronto*," he growled. "Much too fast for a man who's just come into the territory."

Brett shrugged. "Sit down, Sheriff, and cool off. I aim to be around for quite a spell."

"I don't think you will," the lawman countered flatly. "I think you'll be heading back where you came from in less than a week." His voice was as blunt as the finger he jabbed at Brett's wishbone. "I had a talk with Chet Armstrong, soon as I heard what happened on the steps of the Trail House. He didn't say much except that he got what was coming to him. But I'm warning you, Havolin! You go around in this town with that chip on your shoulder, and I'll slam you into the cooler so hard you'll bounce for a week!"

He was big and he had a stubborn honesty that carried weight. But Brett sensed there was more to the ill-concealed hostility in this man's voice than could

21

have been caused by his encounter with Chet Armstrong. He remembered the look on the lawman's face as he regarded Lorna.

A jealous man, Havolin thought. *And dangerous because of it!*

"Tony Mareno was shot to death," Brett said coldly. "You handling that, Sheriff?"

"I am," Ray snapped. "And don't you go around with any fool ideas of doing my job!" He started to turn away, glanced down at the gun tucked inside Brett's waistband. "You stow that hogleg in yore saddle bag when you come to town," he ordered grimly. "Town ordinance."

Brett shrugged.

Something in the redhead's manner annoyed the sheriff. "I'll tell you once more," he said flatly. "Make up yore mind about that two-bit spread you inherited — make it up fast!"

"I may decide to settle here," Brett said coolly.

"I don't think you will!" There was a sneer in the sheriff's voice. He reached out and plucked the last cigar from Brett's breast pocket, passed it under his nose, and bit off an end. "Just to prove my point, I'll buy you a box of these if you last more than a week!"

He turned, chewing on Brett's cigar, and walked out — a hard-fisted man who backed his talk. Brett watched him go, a stubborn smile building around his lips. So far he had learned one thing. No one here cared in the least that Tony Mareno had been murdered — not even the law.

Brett bought a rangy bay with a blaze face at the livery, remembered he had left his saddle in front of the bank and went back for it. A buggy swirled dust over him as he started across the street with it; looking up, he got a glimpse of Lorna Marlin sitting straight on the buggy seat, handling the reins. He stopped and watched her make the turn at the end of River Road where it became a wagon rut angling westward toward the low hills.

Bending, he hitched the saddle up to his shoulder and crossed the street. He went into the livery stable and was saddling the bay when a slight, shifty-eyed man with a pale blond mustache tapped him on the shoulder. Brett swung around fast, his shoulder jamming the man hard against the stall boards. The man grinned nervously.

"Sorry — didn't know you were jumpy," he apologized.

Brett scowled. "Next time make some noise." He looked past the man, seeing no one else. "Want something?"

"Not me." The other shrugged. "Jack Thompson wants to see you."

Brett considered this briefly. Who the devil was Thompson? Then he remembered that Kinsman had mentioned this man as one of the buyers for the Flying Club.

He was about to tell this character that Thompson could come to see him when he remembered that he had received one direct offer so far. Also, he was curious to see what kind of man Thompson was. He was beginning to get really curious as to why four people wanted the Flying Club, which by the measuring rod of this part of Texas was nothing more than a one-horse spread.

He led the bay out of the barn and mounted and followed the small man down the street. Sheriff Hogan was walking south on the opposite side of the road. He stopped and watched Brett and his companion, a thoughtful look in his pale eyes.

Brett tied the bay at the rack of the Palace Bar and went up the two steps behind the thin man. The Palace was a quiet-looking establishment, and the clientele lining the long cherrywood bar were sober townsmen taking a quick one before returning to their places of business.

A big, dark-haired man sat alone at a rear table playing a game of solitaire. He was neatly dressed, and his face was square and almost boyish-looking from a distance. The illusion didn't stand up at close range. The lines around his eyes and his mouth were like the rings in a tree; they told Brett this man was close to fifty.

He stood up across the table as Brett approached. The man who had gone for Brett drifted away toward the bar.

"Sit down," Thompson said pleasantly. He had white even teeth and a nice smile.

"I've got eleven miles to make before the storm breaks. I'll give you two minutes to get out what's on your mind."

Thompson's long fingers flipped a card face up. It was the ace of spades. He looked into Brett's pugnacious face. "If I was superstitious, I'd say this card meant trouble for someone."

Brett moved his shoulders in an impatient gesture. "The name's Brett Havolin," he said curtly.

Thompson nodded. "I know. You're the man Tony Mareno left the Flying Club to."

"I find that seems to have riled more than one of the local citizenry," Brett sneered.

Thompson's brown eyes held amusement. "I also saw you come out of the bank, walk across the street, and drop Chet Armstrong with as smooth a one-two I've ever seen." He chuckled quietly. "A complete stranger, in town for the first time, and you pick on the son of one of the toughest cattlemen in Texas!"

"I'll go back and apologize," Brett snapped. He started to turn away.

Thompson said: "Just a minute, Brett! I asked you here because I wanted to get a good look at you."

"That the only reason you wanted to see me?"

"It is — now," the big man replied. "I wanted to buy the Flying Club — still do," he added quickly. "But you don't look like the kind of man I expected. You don't strike me as the kind who'd sell. Not after finding out that his friend was murdered!"

"Ah!" Brett breathed harshly. "You know that?"

Thompson shrugged. "Don't you?"

Brett shook his head. "Why do you want the Flying Club? A two-bit spread? You don't look like the kind to sweat a living out of a few cows."

"We have that in common," Thompson murmured. "You don't either."

25

"I might fool you," Brett answered. "And you still haven't answered my question."

Thompson picked up his cards. "My reasons are personal," he said. His voice had lost interest. "A means to an end, that's all." He turned a card over, placed it, then met Brett's frowning regard. "I'll top any offer made by the Big Diamond spread," he said quietly. "Remember that, Havolin."

"I'll keep it in mind!" Brett snapped.

He was turning away when Thompson said pleasantly: "No need to go away sore, Brett. The drinks are on me."

Brett looked back. "I'll take you up some other time." He was halfway across the room when Thompson's voice reached him. "If you get into trouble, if you need anything, drop by. No strings, Brett."

There was a thin smile on Thompson's lips, but Brett got the feeling of sincerity in the man. He nodded. Then he turned and pushed his way out to the walk. Mounting the bay, he rode off, following the wagon ruts Lorna had taken a few minutes before.

CHAPTER
THREE

Chet Armstrong peeled his shirt from his muscled torso, dipped a handkerchief in the wash basin and held it to his puffed lips. He kept his eyes on the mirror over the pump handle, and his shoulders twitched as though every word uttered by the big man standing behind him were a bullet tearing through his back.

". . . slammed into the dirt in front of the Trail House, by a man half a foot shorter!" The big man was breathing heavily through his nose. "Shoved around by a pilgrim half yore size! Blast it! What's the Big Diamond coming to?"

"Chet didn't see him," Carol Armstrong said angrily. She had come out of her room into the kitchen, and she was dressed, as always, in a pair of faded blue waist Levis, a checked gingham shirt, half-boots. The pockets of her shirt bobbled as she walked into the room.

"Don't you come around excusing him!" her father flared. "You wiped his nose when he was a button, you fought his battles for him in school. But, Carol, he's supposed to be a man now! Bully Armstrong's boy!"

He gagged, as though the statement choked him.

Lightning flickered through Carol's gray eyes. "If you'd leave him alone, quit riding him —"

Chet turned and put a hard arm on her shoulder, checking her outburst. A forced smile warped his swollen lips. "Take it easy, sis."

She subsided reluctantly..

Bully Armstrong snorted. He was a big man and he looked bigger in this room he had built himself, as he had built everything about the Big Diamond in more than twenty years of hard work. Heavy-framed, wide as a barn door and solid as an oak stump, he seemed as durable as the granite ledge behind the corral and as unyielding. Gray grizzled his brown mane, but the heavy lines that furrowed his face were markers the years had carved.

It took a strong man in this hard country to take what he wanted of it. He had come here when the Cheyennes still raided through Warbonnet Pass, and he had built this place with one hand on an ax handle and the other holding a Spencer carbine.

It was wild country, but he had forced his way on it. He had forced his way on everything he touched, except his own family. His wife had withstood the tempests of his rage, the thrust of his will, yielding a little, bending, but never breaking. She had died with her pride tattered but still flying.

Carol Armstrong had inherited her mother's inner strength. A more robust woman than Ann Armstrong, she had some of the temper of her father. But her will was leavened by a lackadaisical acceptance of the land

and of people, and she had a sensitivity her father did not possess.

Bully Armstrong peered at her from under gray-shot bushy brows. "I heard Prel talking, over by the corral. It'll be all over the Big Diamond by night!" He turned and reached for his hat on a peg by the door. "No one's been man enough to push an Armstrong around in twenty years — no one's starting now! If my son ain't got the guts to settle with this tinhorn, I reckon I'll have to do it for him!"

Carol whirled on him. "Haven't we bullied our way through the valley long enough, Dad? Chet admits he got what he deserved. He shot the man's horse, made him take a bad spill. He thought that would be warning enough to keep snoopers away from the Flying Club — he only did what you told him to!"

Armstrong shook his shaggy head like a riled longhorn pawing the ground. "Right or wrong, that redheaded galoot hit at Big Diamond when he hit Chet. And I ain't being fooled by him, like I wasn't fooled by that other tinhorn, Mareno. Thompson's behind the whole thing. He doesn't dare make an open bid for the Flying Club, because he knows I'd ride out and clean him out if he did. So he sent for Mareno first, and now this hotheaded stranger —"

"Dad!" Carol interrupted. "Think a moment! You've always had your way around here. And you've made your troubles along with it. You're not really certain Tony was hired by Thompson, just like you're not sure about this newcomer. Mareno is dead. I heard he was shot to death." She looked soberly at her father. "Dad, even you aren't big enough to beat murder. Ray Hogan is a stubborn man, and an honest lawman. If Mareno really was shot to death, then Ray's looking for the killer —"

"Shut up!" her father growled.

Carol stood up to him, temper putting color in her cheeks. "You don't frighten me!" she snapped. "You never have!"

He lifted a broad, calloused hand, and she whitened, her lips going bloodless against her teeth. But she didn't flinch from him.

"Don't do it," she said slowly. "I told you what would happen if you ever hit me again!"

He lowered his hand, scowling contemptuously at the stiff set of Chet's face. "Just the same," he growled, "this stranger needs a lesson. The sooner he leaves this country, the smarter an' healthier he'll be!"

"Let me handle him," Carol pleaded. "Just once, let me handle this my way. Maybe I can talk him into leaving — without causing more trouble."

Armstrong hesitated. Then he turned his head, hiding the sudden gleam that flickered through his eyes. "Go ahead," he acquiesced. "I'll give you the chance you've been crying for. If you want to make a fool of yourself —"

He, turned and stamped out, slamming the door behind him.

Brett didn't run into Lorna on the way to the Flying Club. The first splatter of rain kicked up little brown craters in the dust on the road as he turned into the yard. He neck-reined the bay by the pepper tree, his eyes narrowing on the smudge of smoke rising from the chimney. A sleek roan mare that put his stringy bay to shame stood in the shade of the tall pecans which made a cool clump between house and corral.

Brett eased out of saddle, nudged the Colt butt which lay snugged against his hard stomach.

He opened the door and slipped inside the room that was both kitchen and living quarters. He stood quietly, watching the Levi-clad small figure who was bending over the wood range. The smell of freshly brewed coffee made a pleasant tang in the musty air.

She hadn't heard him enter, and he stood there, trying to make sense out of this. This was the girl who had been with Chet Armstrong in Benton Wells.

"Smells real good," he said casually.

The girl started. She turned, and he saw a smudge of wood ash on her cheek. A smile lifted the corners of her mouth, and he saw that her left cheek dimpled.

"Hello," she greeted him. "I didn't find you in when I got here, so I made coffee. Swept up a little, too."

He looked around now, noting that things were cleaner than he remembered them being that morning. He had given the place only a cursory examination, not liking its dinginess.

"Thanks for the maid service," he said. He took his hat off and dropped it over the hook by the door. "What's the catch?"

She said: "I'm Carol Armstrong."

He walked to the stove, looked into the bubbling pot. "I'm Brett Havolin," he answered.

She walked to the cupboard and took down some cups, and he observed dryly: "You seem to know your way around here better than I do."

"Oh, I dropped in on Tony now and then," she said coolly. He raised an eyebrow at this, and she colored. "He was a neighbor," she said defensively, "and a greenhorn in the cattle business."

"And you helped him out?"

Her chin grew firm. "No," she said sharply. "My father owns the Big Diamond Ranch. We run some of our cows this way. During the dry spells we depend some on Piute Creek for water. Mareno's range cut us off, if he wanted to be nasty about it."

"Well, ain't that too bad!" Brett grinned. "Is that why your brother took a shot at me this morning? To keep me from getting nasty?"

"I'm not sure why Chet acted as he did," she answered coldly. Her tone hardened. Obviously she didn't like the way he was jabbing at her, keeping her off verbal balance. "Chet's big, but he isn't rough. Not like Dad. My father keeps after him, bullying him. Maybe Chet thought he would please —" She shrugged. "Why Chet took a shot at you this morning I can't really say. Ask him yourself sometime. But I do know that you humbled him in front of all Benton Wells, and my father won't stand for it. That's why I came to see you — before Dad makes trouble. I want to make amends for Chet, if I may."

There was a sincerity in her tone that almost reached Brett. Tony had been lucky, he thought dryly, to have two beautiful women as close neighbors. Or, he thought grimly, had Tony been lucky after all?

"My account with your brother is settled," he answered levelly. "Except for the matter of a cayuse, which I shall expect payment for."

Carol smiled with evident relief. "I'll see that you get another horse, Mr. Havolin. And —" she stuck out a small brown hand — "I want to be friends."

He took it. The warmth sent a tingling up his arm, and he saw her eyes widen and grow dark. Her smile became uncertain and she pulled her hand away. "I must be riding back. I left my jacket in the other room —"

"Have coffee with me," he invited on the spur of the moment. "I'll ride part way back with you."

She turned in the doorway to the bedroom and smiled. "Thank you. I shall." She disappeared inside, and Brett whistled softly between his teeth. He took the pot off the stove and poured coffee into the cups, using a strainer.

It was unexpectedly homey in here, where he had expected to find only a bleak and shabby room. He wasn't cut out for a hermit's life, and he had not intended to stay here. But he realized now, for the first time in twenty-eight years of bachelorhood, how a woman could change the atmosphere of a place, charge it with a warmth that stirred longings he had not suspected.

The outside door slammed open as he was setting the pot back on the range!

He turned his head, and what he saw snapped the sentimental mood in him. He straightened slowly, his body stiffening at the plain threat of violence emanating from the four men crowding into the room.

The leader was a tall, wiry man of thirty. A dark face, twisted around a puckered scar the size of a quarter in his left cheek. Dark insolent eyes that made a slow, deliberate survey of the room, of Brett Havolin. The pearl handles of two single-action Colts jutted from black leather holsters thonged down on his hips.

The men behind him looked the place over. Carol came to the door then, a brush jacket pulled hastily over one shoulder. Her face was flushed, embarrassed.

"Prel!" she demanded harshly. "What are you doing here?"

Prel kept his eyes on Brett. "In this country, pilgrim," he rasped insolently, "we horsewhip a man for a thing like this!"

Brett cocked an eyebrow at Carol, who was struggling into her jacket. Her face had gone grim. "Prel! Did Dad send you?"

Prel ignored her. He walked toward Brett, and his hands came up swiftly, his guns leveled at Havolin's middle. "Get rid of that Colt, fella!"

Brett eased his Colt out of his waistband and let it fall to the floor. Prel toed it across the room. He was grinning, and his scar made his grin a gargoyle's leer. He kept his dark gaze on Brett as he handed his guns to the man behind him.

"You need a lesson, pilgrim!" His fingers went down to his broad leather belt, unbuckled it, slipped it free.

34

He wrapped one end around his right fist, leaving eighteen inches of leather tipped with the heavy brass buckle swinging free.

"I'm gonna mark that pretty face of yores," he sneered, "so no other woman will ever want to look on it again!"

Carol started across the room. "Prel! If it's the last thing I do I'll make you account for this —"

Prel shoved her into the hands of the short, silent man standing by the wall.

Brett was standing by the stove, feeling the heat from the cast-iron plates against his back. A neat bit of staging, he was thinking bitterly. A trap, baited by a woman!

Prel took a quick step forward and swung. Wrapping that belt around his fist was a mistake he regretted two seconds later. The leather cut through the air toward Brett's face. Havolin stabbed a hand up for the buckle, more in anticipation of stopping that cutting metal than anything else. He felt his palm go numb under the impact; then his fingers closed convulsively and he jerked his arm down.

Prel was yanked off balance. Brett clamped his right arm around Prel's neck, and a primitive savagery was behind his next move. He twisted the squirming Big Diamond ramrod around and deliberately fell with him on the range. He ground Prel's face down on the hot iron plates!

The foreman's scream was a wild, uncontrollable thing. His body squirmed convulsively, broke free. His hands raked for his empty holsters, pain making him momentarily forget; then he turned, clawing for the gun one of his men was lifting from holster.

Brett shouldered Prel roughly around, slammed a fist into Prel's unflexed stomach. He hit him again as the man gagged and started to bend in the middle, and Prel, knocked completely out, fell over backwards.

The quick violence of the incident held the other three men momentarily undecided. They had come to play the part of bystanders, and later of witnesses — this had not been part of the pattern.

Carol slipped free of the open-mouthed man who had been holding her. She glanced down at Prel's unconscious figure, then up at the lanky man who was slowly lifting his gun from holster.

"You use that, Teal," she said grimly, "and I'll kill you!" She was holding the gun she had taken from the short man's holster, and her eyes had a dark, stormy cast.

Teal lowered his Colt.

Carol's gaze shifted to Brett, who smiled bleakly. "Thanks," he said distinctly. "Nice try."

She said miserably: "You think I arranged this, don't you?"

He slid his glance over the hard-faced men in the room. Big Diamond men. "You answer that," he suggested thinly.

She dropped her gaze. "You're a stubborn, ungrateful fool!" she said bitterly. Then she turned. "Teal — you and Bates take Prel outside. Get him back to the ranch as fast as you can. You, Sawdust," she addressed the short, stumpy man who had held her, "ride to Benton

Wells and fetch Doc Blakely. I think Prel is going to need medical attention."

Brett watched them haul the moaning Big Diamond ramrod to his feet, carry him outside. The rain was pattering heavily against the pitched roof. But the warmth had gone out of this room and the coffee was no longer inviting.

Carol faced him. "Believe what you like," she said defiantly. "But I did come as a friend, because there's been too much of Big Diamond power antagonizing peaceful people here. Because," her eyes softened, and a miserable look sneaked in, "I'm tired of being called Bully Armstrong's daughter —"

He said nothing, and her shoulders stiffened as she turned, walked out. Brett waited until he heard her cayuse move away. Then he rubbed his bruised knuckles across his jaw and turned with soured anticipation to his coffee.

CHAPTER
FOUR

Brett lay awake a long time, listening to the steady beat of the rain. The roof leaked down near the fieldstone chimney, and the steady dripping fed his gray mood.

Tony had lived here, alone, for almost nine months. Brett couldn't believe it. Not Tony, who worked hard and played harder. A woman in every town in East Texas.

Oil had been Tony's business, and his. They had been saving, that last year, for the time they'd wildcat on their own. A lease and a well — the dream of every man who mucked around the oil fields that were springing up around the Big Spindle well.

His thoughts came around to Lorna Marlin, and he recalled one of Tony's few letters, trying now to analyze it in the light of what he had encountered here.

". . . found the girl, if she'll have me. Lives with her widowed mother across the creek. A nice neighbor. You'll like Lorna Marlin, Brett. Not like the girls you're used to. She's got class . . ."

Yet Lorna had not seemed to share Tony's hopes. She had barely acknowledged knowing him. Carol Armstrong had been franker. Brett frowned. Too frank. Yet Tony had never mentioned her. Why?

He got up and shuffled into the kitchen. His bare feet recoiled from the runnel of water caused by the leak around the chimney. He felt for the coffee pot, decided against it.

Darn Tony, he thought peevishly. But he knew he couldn't leave without finding out who had killed him. Brett had a streak of stubbornness. And he and Tony had been as close as brothers.

Four people wanted the Flying Club — a shack with a leaky roof and a few hundred acres of graze land.

Carol had made it plain why Bully Armstrong wanted it. But what about the others?

Lorna? She had evaded a direct answer.

Thompson? The gambler had kept his reasons to himself.

Walter Baggett, president of the bank? Maybe Baggett wanted to go into the cattle business. But why buy the Flying Club?

He felt the need of a smoke, but he had run out of cigars and had neglected to buy more in town. He turned in finally, remembering Lorna's invitation. "Drop by sometime, Brett."

Dawn was a dismal grayness that spread across the wet sky. Havolin rose early and drew water from the pump well outside, brought it back in an oak bucket. He poured some into a tin pan and warmed it on the stove and shaved.

The bruise on his nose stood out, and his upper lip was tender as he scraped the red stubble. His eyes were blue-gray, and somehow they reminded him of Carol's. He finished, wiped his face dry.

He walked to the door, looked out. The pecan trees dripped. The corral was still empty. He didn't know if the Flying Club had had any stock at the time of Tony's death; he would have to ask Kinsman about it. The yard edged out to the narrow trail angling across a low hill, shutting off sight of Piute Creek. There was nothing in sight as far as he could see, and he shook his head, feeling the sharp loneliness of a man used to people and towns.

Turning back to the kitchen, he stopped, unaccountably feeling again the presence of the slim figure bending over the range, and the memory had the ability to bring back a bit of warmth to the bleak room.

He grinned crookedly as he walked to the stove, reheated last night's coffee. He didn't cook breakfast; he didn't even look to see if there was food in the cupboard. He didn't intend to stay here any longer than necessary, but he wasn't going to advertise the fact that he was leaving. Not until he found out who had killed Tony Mareno. And why.

Somehow he felt this was very important.

The coffee gave him a lift. He walked out to the barn and saddled the bay and rode out of the yard. On the hill, he looked across the creek, spotting the small curl of smoke rising from the Marlin place.

He made it in less than a half-hour. The Marlin place was no bigger than the Flying Club. But there was a difference. There were curtains in the two windows facing the yard, flower beds in front of it. There was a neatness here that only women could impress on a place. A milk cow mooed from a small, enclosed pasture, and two staked-out goats turned to stare at him with whiskered dignity.

Brett rode into the yard and stepped out of saddle. He knocked on the door and a soft voice acknowledged him. He had his hat in his hand as he stepped inside.

The soft voice was not Lorna's. It belonged to a small, wispy woman with iron gray hair, a motherly face. She was in a wheel chair, a shawl across her lap, her hands folded. The room had cloth rugs on the floor, pictures on the walls, and it reminded Brett of his own home he had left more than thirteen years ago.

"Good morning, son," the woman said. She had a gentle voice, and her eyes blinked behind steel-rimmed spectacles. Brett's glance shifted to the heavy Sharps rifle that hung on pegs above the fireplace. It seemed out of place in that room.

"You must be the young man Lorna spoke of," the woman said. "Our new neighbor."

He nodded, feeling at ease here. "Brett Havolin, ma'am."

"I'm Mady Marlin." She smiled tremulously. "I'm so glad you called, Mr. Havolin. We seldom have visitors, you know. Lorna will be glad to see you."

He glanced toward the curtained doorway which he guessed led to a bedroom, and Mrs. Marlin, catching the look, shook her head. "My daughter's an early riser. You'll find her down by the creek, by the clump of jackpine yonder. Run along and fetch her. I'll have breakfast for you both when you return."

He put a questioning glance on her, and she smiled. "Oh, I get around a little. But I tire easily —"

41

Brett fingered his hat. "Thank you," he murmured. He knew now why Tony had liked it here. He closed the door and looked down the creek. The sun was out and beginning to warm the wet land, and the freshness in the clean air was like a tonic, making him hungry.

He walked toward the pine clump, found what looked like a well-used path, and followed it.

Lorna stopped before they reached the house, on the small knoll on the edge of the pine grove. She nuzzled his shoulder, her voice warm and intimate. "I wanted you to sell the Flying Club to me. But now I'd much rather you stayed —"

"I'll think about it," he said carelessly. He ran his knuckles gently across the back of her neck and then pulled her to him. Her lips were warm and eager.

"Mother needs me, Brett. I'm all she lives for —" She broke away, breathing quickly. "I don't want to hurt her. I want you to understand her. My mother lives most of the time in dreams. The Ollivans, her surname before she married my father, were well-to-do folk in North Carolina. She married Dad — he was from West Virginia — and came west with him. She had great hopes. But he died the year after he settled here. She had too much pride to go back home."

Brett said: "I've met your mother, Lorna. And I like her." But he felt slightly embarrassed as they walked to the house. Lorna opened the door, and the smell of bacon crisping sharpened his dormant hunger.

He had breakfast with them, marveling at the way the slight, sharp-eyed woman talked, as though he were already an old and trusted friend. It made him uneasy.

Mady Marlin often wandered off the subject at hand. She talked of beaus and dates and soft Carolina moons, and the transitions were sharp and without warning. Lorna's eyes, meeting his at these moments, would flash their quick appeal.

"Please come again, Mr. Havolin," Mrs. Marlin invited. "You're our nearest neighbor, you know — and it is often lonely here. Lorna has so much to do in town."

He nodded his acceptance. Lorna remained in the doorway, beside her mother, waving goodbye as he rode away . . .

He crossed the creek and then, not relishing the prospect of returning to the dismal shack he had inherited, he took a wide swing westward. The Flying Club, he saw, lay in a natural flat, ringed on the north and east by a sandstone formation. Beyond it the land faded to dry country of lonely buttes.

The Big Diamond spread lay behind his shack, its acres dominating the valley. He rode all morning, swinging in a wide arc about the main ranch buildings, avoiding the few riders he saw at a distance. But he was able to make out that the Big Diamond was a rambling spread, seemingly made up of numerous sheds and out-buildings. The main house seemed no more pretentious than the buildings surrounding it. In fact, the barn, painted a vivid green, seemed to dominate the conglomeration of structures and corrals.

He saw Big Diamond cattle everywhere . . .

It was well past noon when he jogged his tired bay into the Flying Club ranchyard. Unsaddling in the small barn, he walked back to the house and saw that he had had visitors.

The note tacked to his door was bluntly worded: *"Get out of this country pronto, Havolin!"*

He tore the note down and crumpled it and tossed it aside. Then he went inside, hung his hat on the hook by the door. He rifled the cupboard and found a few meager cans. Beans and tomatoes and peaches. A small sack of flour had provided sustenance for rodents before it got moldy. Potatoes had sprouted eyes and withered.

He cleaned out the cupboard. He found coffee in a small earthenware jug protected by a cover, and he brought it to the stove and set to work lighting a fire. With the wood burning, he set water on the plates to boil. He felt hungry and a little baffled. He had never prepared his own food, and he didn't like the thought that he would have to learn to cook or ride eleven miles to town for a restaurant meal.

He wondered briefly how Tony had made out. Tony hadn't been able to flip himself an egg before leaving Beaumont.

He was hacking open a can of peaches, the smell of coffee strong in the room, when he heard a rider. He stepped away from the table and was ready when the visitor opened the door.

Carol froze, staring at the gun in Brett's hand!

44

He said not too pleasantly: "You sure make yourself at home here. I don't remember inviting you back."

She flushed. She was a quick-tempered girl ordinarily, but somehow his words, backed by the bitter truth, pushed her off balance.

"I had hoped you'd cooled off by now," she said. "I came back to tell you that I had nothing to do with what happened yesterday. I didn't know that Prel and the others followed me. Dad had promised to let me handle it my way."

He grinned coldly. "So it wasn't a friendly visit, was it? Your dad sent you first, then his strong-arm men!"

Her cheeks reddened. "You are a muleheaded, conceited fool!" she said angrily. "You're more stubborn than my father, and maybe you'll deserve what you'll get!"

Brett's anger rose to match hers. "Get what Tony got?" he asked harshly.

Mention of Tony's death seemed to take the props from under her indignation. Her shoulders slumped. "I liked Tony. I want you to believe that. And I didn't know, until very recently, that he had been shot. I can't imagine who would want to kill him —"

Brett sneered. "There have been four people interested in buying this place since I arrived here. Look around you, Miss Armstrong. What's so valuable about this property? A ramshackle log cabin, a barn, a corral. What's on it? Gold?"

She answered quietly, "I don't know why anyone would want this place — except to live here. It does have possibilities —"

"For what?"

"For living!" Her eyes suddenly flashed. "Tony wanted that. He told me once that was why he had left east Texas. He said he thought he had found what he wanted out here."

"Tony told you that?" Brett asked, unbelieving. "He confided in you that much?" He shook his head. "Yet he never once mentioned you in his letters to me."

Carol's shoulders were straight. "That was his privilege, Mr. Havolin."

"It sure was," Brett answered callously. "And in case you're interested, your father is the only one who has threatened me since I came to this section. And after what happened last night you can hardly blame me for taking a rather dim view of the Big Diamond."

She shook her head. "I didn't come back to apologize for Dad. He's run this valley so long he'll always consider it his private domain. But he would leave you alone if he could be sure you weren't a Thompson man."

"I'll write him a letter!" Brett snapped. He walked up to her, his face hard, his stubbornness dominating him. "Or won't that be enough? What proof, what assurance, does your father really want?"

"I don't know!" Carol cried. "I only came to help." She dropped her hands to her sides in a hopeless gesture.

She looked small and tired and helpless, and he felt her need in that moment, almost the sort of need of reassurance a small child has. He put his hands on her shoulders, and he felt her tremble and instinctively he pulled her to him. His lips went down to meet hers, and he found them unexpectedly soft and yielding and fresh . . .

She pulled away with a start, her eyes wide and startled. He made no move toward her, and she whirled and ran for the door. Brett still tasted the sweetness of her lips as the sound of her departure faded into the afternoon stillness . . .

CHAPTER
FIVE

Slowly Brett walked back to the stove, absently poured himself a cup of coffee from the bubbling pot. But the brew tasted bitter, and he felt restless and unsatisfied. He walked to the door and flung it open and looked past the pecans to the road that led to town.

Clouds moved like dirty cotton wads across the blue sky. The wind, coming up from the west, had a clean keen bite.

What in blazes did a man do out here? he thought irritatedly. He looked around the place, trying to fathom what had decided Tony Mareno to settle here, trying to understand what had kept him here. What had Tony done with his days?

He spotted the wagon under the lean-to shed at the far end of the corral, and curiosity drew him to it. A little spring wagon, it had been recently painted a medium green. A board in the wagon bed had been replaced. Harness hung on pegs on the walls.

Brett went into the barn. Several hens, living on borrowed time, ran squawking from a small pile of hay stacked in a far corner. He stopped in the middle of the hard-packed earth floor and surveyed the double stalls at one end of the barn. His cayuse moved restlessly in one, turning his head to look at him. A short ladder led up to an open-fronted loft where more hay and several bags of grain were stored. Rodents had made inroads in one of the bags.

Brett shook his head. He still couldn't fit Tony Mareno into this picture.

He remembered seeing magazines on the small table in Tony's bedroom. He had given them only a cursory glance, but several of the titles came to mind now. *The Stockman's Gazette. The Breeder's Manual.*

Tony must have been serious about all this, he thought dismally. He walked out of the barn and paused under the biggest of the pecans. Frayed lengths of old rope hung from a thick branch, almost brushing his face. The ground under his feet was scooped out in a shallow trench, and the thought came to him that there had been a swing here once — and children. Possibly children of the man from whom Tony had bought the spread.

The sun filtered through the whispering leaves, touching his face. What was it Carol Armstrong had said? "I don't know why anyone would want this place — except to live here."

He stared off into space, unconsciously making a comparison between Carol and Lorna Marlin. Despite her air of self-reliance, the Armstrong girl was still young and naïve — all her hopes and her strength, her desires and her dreams were still locked in her, waiting for the right man to release them. There was a promise in her that Brett sensed — had felt in the touch of her lips.

The other was a woman, a woman who would give of herself only enough to get what she needed . . .

Tony had lived here nine months. He had known both Carol and Lorna. Slowly Brett started to walk back to the cabin. That, too, was something about Tony he had not suspected. It seemed to him unbelievable that Tony Mareno had not made the same discovery he had.

He became aware then of the rider on the road from town. Brett straightened, casting aside his brooding thoughts. He had not come to take the place of Tony Mareno here.

The newcomer did not seem at home in his saddle. He rode somewhat stiffly, taking the jolts badly. He was near enough now for Brett to see that he was a slender, neatly dressed man in a gray town suit, expensive pearl gray Stetson, hand-stitched half-boots.

The rider pulled up at the turn-in to the Flying Club and waved. Brett waited, not answering the greeting. He did not know the man, and now he wasn't sure that this man was headed for the Flying Club. The wagon road, he recalled, kept on, cutting through the thicket of scrub oak on the small hill and crossing the creek to the Marlin place.

The rider hesitated, then made a decision. He swung his horse over and cantered toward Brett. Havolin waited.

The townsman reined in a few feet from Brett. He was a good-looking slim man in his early thirties. Clean-shaven, with dark, quick gray eyes. A touch of gray at his temples lent a dignified air to his bearing.

50

His voice was soft and pleasant. It reminded Brett of the gambler, Jack Thompson.

"I'm Walter Baggett," he introduced himself, "of the Bank of Gibraltar in town." He relaxed, leaning over his saddle horn, his smile friendly. "You're Brett Havolin?"

Brett nodded. "Light," he invited. "There's coffee on the fire."

The banker shook his head. "Thanks, anyway." He ran a brief glance over the house and outbuildings behind Havolin. "I'm on my way to visit with the Marlins. Saw you standing here and dropped by to say hello."

Brett remembered Lawyer Kinsman's list of prospective buyers. "I heard you wanted to buy the place. You still making an offer?"

Baggett shook his head. "I did tell Kinsman I would be interested," he admitted. He made a gesture with his hand. "Nice place for relaxation; perhaps some fishing. That's all I had in mind. However, I've since heard you've received several other offers, no doubt much more attractive than I could offer you." His smile was rueful. "I have no intention of going into the cattle business, Havolin."

"Neither have I."

The banker shrugged. "There's a rumor going around town that Tony's death wasn't an accident."

"It's a strange rumor," Brett admitted. "Your sheriff admitted Tony was shot to death."

Baggett shook his head. "Just goes to show you. Up to this morning I thought Tony's death was the result of an accidental tumble into Piute Creek, just above white water. He used to go there often, I heard, to fish." His glance roved curiously over the empty corral. "Are you planning to settle down here?"

"No."

"Stay long?"

"Long enough to find out who killed Tony."

The slender townsman frowned. "But who would have wanted to kill him? He was a pleasant chap, as I recall. He seemed well liked in town. Of course, he did have some trouble with Big Diamond, but —" Baggett let his glance slide over the house and outbuildings again, as if trying to find something he might have overlooked. "Surely," he took up wonderingly, "there's not enough here to tempt anyone into murder."

Brett's voice was level. "I'm not sure of that, Mr. Baggett."

The town man's eyes jerked back to meet his. They held a hard, expectant glint. "Ah! Perhaps you've found out something, Havolin? Something that would account for your other offers? Gold?"

"Maybe."

Baggett waited, and Brett sensed that the man was tensed and eager. Then, when Brett remained silent, Baggett eased. "Well," he said politely, "I hope you have more luck with this place than Tony had."

Havolin watched the banker ride off. *Maybe it is gold,* he thought grimly. *Whatever it is, you know what is here. And I think you're a liar about not wanting the place now.*

52

There were too many people who wanted to buy the Flying Club, he reflected cynically, for diverse and seemingly innocent reasons.

He let his thoughts run on this thread, but he reached no conclusive answers. Someone had killed Tony either for personal reasons, which seemed unlikely from the general consensus of liking for Tony which Brett had encountered here, or because someone had found something of value about the Flying Club and had hoped, with Tony's death, to take possession.

That was as far as Havolin got. Then, because he was an active man, not given to contemplation, he turned to the house. He was hungry, and though it seemed ridiculous to have to ride eleven miles to town for a meal, he saw no other alternative.

Tony's brush jacket was still hanging on a hook on the bedroom door. Brett took it down, remembering that he and Tony had much the same build, had often swapped clothes. Getting into Tony's jacket seemed entirely natural, and he gave it no further thought.

It was late afternoon when he rode into Benton Wells. He stopped by the general store first and bought a handful of cigars. The owner, a graying, spectacled man named Tobey Orrin, was affable. He knew who Brett was, and he made a point of telling Havolin that Tony Mareno had traded here.

"An easygoing young man," he told Brett, counting out Brett's change. "Came here green as a fresh-skun hide, bought out Phil Rodman's place. Phil was pretty discouraged. Wife was ailing, and when his oldest boy lost his leg in a hunting accident —" The storekeeper shook his head. "Phil was muleheaded, though. He could have sold out to Bully Armstrong — but he claimed he wouldn't be strongarmed by any man. So he sold out to Tony, for less than Armstrong would have paid him." He chuckled softly. "Sure riled old Bully Armstrong —"

Brett cut off the garrulous man. "Riled him enough, perhaps, to make him take it out on the new owner? On Tony?"

Orrin blinked. "Not that way, no sir," he said hastily. "Heard him say myself that Tony wasn't bothering him. In fact —" he paused and licked his lips — "it was Armstrong's daughter who sent away for subscriptions to a bunch of cattle-raising magazines for Tony."

Brett grinned coldly. "Right neighborly," he admitted. He picked up his change, and Orrin asked: "You coming to the dance Saturday night?"

"Dance?"

"Big Diamond shindig in the courthouse. Bully Armstrong treats every year." The storeman's voice was dry. "Biggest thing in Benton Wells, Mr. Havolin. More young-uns get hitched in the next week than in the rest of the year. Cause of more scandals, too —"

Brett cut him off again. "I'll try to make it," he nodded.

He started to leave, then remembered his nearly empty larder at the Flying Club. He picked out a number of items, mostly canned goods, a slab of bacon, a jug of molasses.

"Put it in a flour sack," he said. "I'll be by for it later."

54

He rode down the street to the livery stable and turned his cayuse over to the hostler. He wanted to walk, burn up some of his restlessness. He was getting nowhere in Tony's case. Maybe the sheriff was right — it was the law's business. He couldn't help Tony now. If he had any sense he'd take the highest offer and head back for Beaumont.

But somehow that thought settled nothing. He stopped walking and lighted a cigar and tried to analyze his reluctance. *You darned fool!* he berated himself. *You falling for Tony's sentimental streak? Next thing you know you'll be staying here, reading books on cattle raising!*

He bit through his cigar, spat out the shredded tobacco and tossed the smoke into the street.

"I'll wire Morrison now," he muttered, "before I get a touch of brain fever."

He found the telegraph office combined with the stage station on the corner of River Road and Coyote Street. The telegrapher read the message back to Brett: "Sam Morrison, care of Parker House, Beaumont, Texas. Decided to join you on Selwyn lease. Expect me in ten days. Brett Havolin."

Havolin paid for the message and went out, feeling better than he had since his arrival. He took another cigar from his pocket and lighted up, and was about to head up River Road for Polly's Restaurant when he saw Kinsman. The attorney had just stepped out of the Dusty Hole and was teetering on his heels, obviously having trouble deciding which way to navigate.

Brett joined him before he made up his mind. The lawyer swayed to windward, recovered his balance, and jabbed a forefinger against Brett's chest. "You owe me a hundred simoleons —"

Havolin slipped a cigar between Kinsman's teeth. "Bite on this," he grinned. "You listen better with your mouth shut."

Kinsman spluttered indignantly, but he kept a firm bite on the cigar. "You're a high-handed cuss!" he accused. "Should have known better than to have dealings with a redheaded fool like you. Any man who'd tangle with that mean-faced Big Diamond foreman, Prel, ain't got —"

"Whoa!" Brett said sharply. "Where'd you hear that?"

The attorney grinned waggishly. "Ain't much goes on I don't hear about —"

Brett took his arm and turned him in the direction of his office. "I want to talk to you."

Kinsman held back. "Do I get my hundred simoleons?"

"When you earn it."

Kinsman snorted. But he followed Brett to his office, navigating the steep flight with Brett's help. At the door he shrugged Brett's hand off, pushed the door open and headed immediately for his desk. He pulled open the left top drawer, carefully lifted out a half filled bottle of whiskey. His groping fingers found a glass, and he poured a generous two fingers, slopping a little on the desk top.

"For my client," he said, waving generously. "I'll use the bottle."

He tilted it to his lips, took a long pull, withdrawing the bottle with an audible sound of satisfaction.

"Now," he said, wiping his lips with the back of his sleeve, "what's on your mind, son?"

Brett walked up to him, pushed him gently down into a chair and took the bottle out of his hand.

"We'll start with the first thing," he said. "Tony wrote me he was doing some farming and some stock raising. Mentioned Herefords and some Whitefaces. I don't know what he was talking about, Kinsman. I'm not a cattle man." Havolin placed the bottle on the desk and made a gesture with his hands. "There's nothing up there now except an empty corral, a garden patch gone to weeds — some chickens. I want to know what happened to this stock Tony was raising."

Kinsman leaned back, pursed his thick lips. "Strayed, maybe," he mumbled. "Heck!" he burst out peevishly. "I was his lawyer, not his handy man. Sure, Tony had about forty head. Good beef. Ranged them east of his place — on grass Big Diamond claims is theirs. Might be that Bully Armstrong claimed them, too."

He straightened up at the look on Brett's face. "Now wait a minute, son! Don't be a consarned idiot! I'm not claiming that Big Diamond did take over Tony's cows. Armstrong's got a lot of faults, and he ain't much liked around here. But he's too big to fool around with forty head belonging to another man —"

"He seems big enough to do what he wants around here!" Brett snapped.

Kinsman let that pass. "Tony had two saddle horses which he sometimes used for his wagon. Both chestnuts, but one has a blaze face. They're down at Baker's Livery. You can claim them by paying the feed bill."

"Why didn't you tell me that yesterday?"

"You didn't ask me!" Kinsman snapped. "And you were too blamed cocksure for a stranger who'd just blown into town!"

Brett's smile was a little sheepish. "Reckon I was at that," he admitted. He took another cigar from his pocket and tossed it on the desk. "On account," he said coldly. "You'll get your hundred later, the day I sell the Flying Club."

Kinsman blinked owlishly. "Decided to take my advice?"

"Why not? It's too late to help Tony — and I wasn't out to be a farmer." Brett started to leave, stopped, looked back at Kinsman who was reaching for the bottle. "By the way, Tony couldn't recognize the right end of a skillet when I knew him. He couldn't have eaten all his meals in town."

Kinsman ran the tips of his fingers over his nose. "Tony was a likable young fellow," he pointed out. "And the Marlins, I hear, are right neighborly people. From Virginia, I heard."

Brett nodded shortly. "I got you."

He walked down the long flight of stairs and paused on the edge of the plank walk, still turning over in his mind Kinsman's last remark. The Marlins were neighborly all right — he had had a sample of their hospitality himself. He wondered if Lorna had used the same tactics on Tony — and for the same reasons.

58

Standing there, looking down the quiet, tree-shaded street, Brett had the discouraging thought that he would never know why Tony had been killed. Sure, Tony had been well liked. Brett heard that everywhere. But his death seemed to have been forgotten too quickly. Brett had the feeling that people hereabouts wanted to avoid thinking about it.

The evening shadows were lengthening across the road. The thought of eating dinner and then riding back to that empty cabin depressed him. He toyed with the thought of taking a room in the Trail House.

He ate in Polly's, and was surprised to find he was less hungry than he had thought. Coming out to the walk, he saw Sheriff Hogan stop across the street and look at him. The rangy lawman stood out among the others moving on the walk.

The sheriff's holstered Colt, a bone-handled Peacemaker, reflected a glint of light and reminded Brett that he had left his Colt at the Flying Club. If Hogan wanted to check on him, he was welcome, he thought humorlessly.

But the sheriff turned and walked away, and Brett headed in the other direction. He was more than half decided now that he would stay in town tonight. He needed a drink. He wanted to feel a night crowd around him again, play a little poker, maybe. He wasn't cut out to be a farmer — to settle down. Not while Sam Morrison waited for him in Beaumont — not while there was the chance of wildcatting a strike that would make him rich overnight.

He headed for the Trail House with a dangerous glint in his eye. A half-dozen horses nosed the rail of the Tin Cup Saloon. A burst of raucous, demanding voices spilled through the slatted doors. Brett paused to make out the brand on the nearest cayuse. Big Diamond!

Impulse had its way with him. Big Diamond seemed to be running things in this section. He was curious to see the man who was Big Diamond — the man known as Bully Armstrong.

He turned and went up the stairs. Light splashed through the slatted doors, making its pattern on the boards. He was in this light when a shadowy figure queried softly: "Havolin?"

Brett turned. He glimpsed the downward movement of the man's hand. Then the night exploded into a blaze of pinwheeling lights that burned out to an inky blackness . . .

CHAPTER
SIX

A steady jolting hurt the back of Brett's head. The pain behind his eyes was the first thing of which he was aware. He squeezed them shut, but the throbbing remained. After a while he opened his eyes. He knew they were open, but he couldn't see a thing. Fear laid its hand on him then, overriding the throbbing in his head. A cold sweat chilled him.

He tried to bring his hands to his eyes, and only then did he realize that they were tied. So were his feet.

Awareness came faster now. He was on his back, with his bound hands under him. The jolting movement of whatever he was lying on finally identified itself as a wagon bed. A canvas tarp had been pulled over him, blanking out his vision. He could feel its rough texture now as he probed at it with his chin.

He listened, anger crawling through him, brushing aside his initial fear. The wagon, it seemed, was not alone on its journey. Riders flanked it. Brett heard the soft scuffing of leather above the whirring wagon wheels, an occasional clang of shod hoofs on imbedded rocks. One of the riders kept whistling "Johnny Reb" off key.

The wagon jolted heavily now over some road-bed obstruction. The driver cursed, and someone riding flank laughed unsympathetically.

"Thought you could drive this road in the dark, Teal," the same voice jeered.

The driver's answer was a thin cursing.

A half-hour later — it seemed much more to the angry man inside the wagon — a harsh voice said: "This is good enough, Teal."

The wagon stopped. The driver fastened his reins, turned in his seat. He pulled the tarp from Brett's face and looked down into Brett's blazing eyes. He grunted, called back over his shoulder: "He's wide awake, boss, an' riled as a treed bobcat!"

"Get him out!" the harsh voice ordered.

Teal took a clasp knife from his pants pocket, snapped the big blade open, and cut the rope from around Brett's legs. Then he rolled Havolin on his face and sawed his hands free. Straightening, he closed his knife and slid it into his pocket.

"All right, buster," he growled. "This is where you get out."

Rage had been building up in Brett with the passing miles, a wild and heedless rage. He flexed his hands, feeling the blood come back into them, feeling the pin-pricks of pain in his fingers. He drew his legs up under him, got his palms on the wagon bed, and came up fast. His shoulder piled into Teal's stomach, toppling the man over the side.

Teal's squawk of alarm was cut short as he landed heavily.

Brett straightened, planting his feet wide. The wagon, he saw, had stopped in a small clearing, ringed by shadowy trees. A high riding slice of moon provided enough light for Havolin to make out the half-dozen riders ringing him.

He saw Prel first, sitting slack in saddle. The Big Diamond foreman's dark face was swathed in bandages that gleamed whitely against the shadows. Chet Armstrong was there, beside an enormously broad man who sat solidly in saddle of a big blue roan. Brett didn't recognize the others.

"Still got a lot of fight in him," the broad man observed. He seemed amused and a little pleased.

Teal came to his feet and reached for the knife in his pocket. Bully Armstrong's voice stopped him, ordered him away from the wagon. Then he rode up close to the wagon and made a gesture with his thumb. "Get down, Red!"

Havolin didn't move. He slid his glance to the reins tied to the brake handle and wondered if he could make a break through those riders circling the wagon.

Armstrong eased his Colt from holster. "Get down!" he repeated harshly.

Havolin climbed down. The effort started the heavy pounding in his head again, and he felt his stomach turn over. A sudden weakness in his knees made him lean back against the wagon.

Armstrong slid his Colt back into its holster and started unbuckling his cartridge belt.

"For a stranger here you've been right proddy, hombre," he said grimly. "Five minutes in town an' you're tanglin' with my son. Before the day is over you're gettin' free with my daughter —"

"Dad!" Chet's voice held angry impatience. "You know why he —"

"Shut up!" Bully Armstrong's voice was like a whip. Chet caught his anger, choked back on it. He had obeyed this big man's voice for years, and habit was a strong thing for him to break.

Havolin pushed away from the wagon wheel against which he had rested. He stood slack-armed, facing the broad, powerful boss of Big Diamond. He forced an insolence he didn't feel at the moment into his smile.

"You forget Prel," he said bleakly.

"I never forget anything!" Armstrong snapped. He slid his cartridge belt free and handed it to his son. "I'm twice your age, Havolin. But I'm goin' to give you the beatin' of your life!"

He stepped down from his roan, hooked his big Stetson on the horn, and turned to face Brett. He spat on his horny hands and rubbed his palms together in grim anticipation.

"What are you waitin' for?" he jeered, shuffling forward. "Want me to —"

Havolin stepped in and hit Armstrong, smearing the burly man's mouth with blood. The blow rocked Armstrong back on his heels, and Brett tried to follow through. But he was slow. The first blow he struck hurt him almost as much as it did Armstrong. He felt the jarring impact start the heavy, nauseating pounding in his head. The pain seemed to squeeze his eyes shut, and his left hand glanced off Armstrong's ear.

That was the last blow he struck.

Armstrong's left hand cuffed his next blow aside. Brett was off balance when the Big Diamond boss's fist split his lips, sent him reeling back against the wagon. The wheel rim pressed against his back; it helped keep him on his feet. The pain in his head was a blinding, unbearable thing. He put out his hands to ward off Armstrong's blows — he tried to lunge away from the wagon.

Deliberately the burly cattle boss slugged him, in the head, shoulders, ribs, stomach. Havolin sagged, started to slide down along the wheel. Armstrong's last blow caught him under the left ear, dropping him in a crumpled, unconscious heap.

The Big Diamond boss stood over Brett, spitting blood from his cut mouth. He looked disappointed.

"Cripes!" he growled. "I barely worked up a sweat."

No one in the silent group behind him commented. Armstrong walked back to his horse, jammed his hat on his head, climbed into saddle. He held out a hand for his gunbelt, and Chet handed it to him.

"Let's go home!" Armstrong ordered. His voice held the finality of a man whose work was done.

Chet said: "What about him?" He indicated the unconscious man.

"It's a five-mile walk back to town!" his father snapped. "If he's got the brains of a muley calf, he'll take the first stage back to where he came from." He reached inside his hip pocket for a blue, polka-dotted handkerchief and wiped blood from his lips. He flung a look at the red-head.

"Tough, eh? Why, he wilted faster than last year's daisies, Chet!"

He waited until Teal had climbed into the wagon seat, then made an authoritative gesture with his arm. He rode across the clearing, the others falling in around the wagon. They rode west, across bumpy ground, the wagon jolting and lurching over the rough spots. When they finally hit the road to the Big Diamond Prel reined his animal aside.

"Going back to town, boss," he said loudly. "Just remembered I'm fresh out of the makings."

Armstrong grunted his assent. He didn't look back at his foreman. The others kept on with him, flanking the wagon. Even before the Big Diamond foreman received the burn on his face he had been a hard man to get along with — now he was intolerable. Most of them were glad to see him turn back, fade into the darkness.

But Chet Armstrong kept seeing Havolin's crumpled figure in the clearing. Slowly he let his mount fall behind the others . . .

Brett Havolin rolled over and painfully pushed himself to his hands and knees. His whole body ached. He remained on his knees, sucking in air against his bruised rib cage. His tongue probed his thickened, cut lips.

The Big Diamond riders had gone, taking the wagon with them. At the moment he was too hurt to care. His head ached again from the gun butt that had raised the egg-sized lump over his left ear.

66

He was sick and hurt and he had been badly whipped by a man twice his age — and the humiliation touched off a grim and deadly anger in him. Armstrong had run the valley for twenty years by such methods — by guns and fists. Whatever his reasons, he, Havolin, had been considered just another minor obstacle in Armstrong's way — an obstacle to be roughly shoved aside.

Deep inside Brett an insolent pride asserted itself. Ever since he had come to Benton Wells he had been advised, ordered and manhandled to get him to leave. And the Big Diamond had been doing most of the ordering!

He pushed himself to his feet and stood swaying, fighting the sickness that clawed at his stomach. On rubbery legs he walked to a rock on the edge of the clearing and sat down. He bent forward with his hand between his knees, and his dinner came up and he lost it.

The night wind was cool across his face, chilling the sweat on his brow. But he felt better, clearer-headed. He got up, his mouth tightening against the pain that racked his body.

He had no idea how far he had been taken from town, nor in which direction to walk. But he was a stubborn man, as Bully Armstrong would find out.

His hat made a black blotch beside the wagon ruts. Havolin walked slowly to it, bent carefully, and picked it up. He was straightening when he heard a horseman come riding toward the clearing.

He turned to face the newcomer, hope lifting his hurt spirits. Hope died the moment the shadowy rider emerged into the clearing and reined in.

For an interval there was only the silence of the night. Prel let the moment drag out, relishing it. Then he drew his Colt. He palmed it without any hurry, snicking the spiked hammer back with his thumb.

"This is my score, Havolin," he said. His voice, partially muffled by his bandages, had a mocking note. "But it'll have a Big Diamond tag. Another tally on the wrong side of Bully Armstrong's book."

Havolin's fists clenched. "I pegged you for a polecat, Prel!" he said desperately, "but not as yellow. Toss me a gun —"

"Why?" Prel edged his cayuse around until he was almost broadside to the redhead. "I came back to kill you, Havolin, not to —"

He jerked around, clearly surprised, as a rider broke through the shadows behind him. His teeth showed in a startled grimace. He brought his gun hand across his chest and snapped a shot at the horseman breaking into the clearing. He thumbed another in desperate haste, and the return blast doubled him up. He fired his last shot blindly, almost into the ear of his panicky horse. The animal reared and screamed, and Prel fell loosely, hitting the ground like a sack of meal.

Havolin didn't move. He saw the man who had killed Prel ride slowly forward into the pale slanting moonlight.

Chet Armstrong!

It didn't make sense to him. Nor did Chet's bitter voice help. "I owe you a cayuse, Havolin. Take Prel's. It's a Big Diamond animal. And get out of this country!"

Havolin walked slowly forward. He stopped by Prel's body. The Big Diamond foreman's cayuse, a rangy

68

steeldust, had stopped a few feet away. Frowning, Brett looked up at Chet.

"You speaking for yourself, or for Bully Armstrong?"

"For both!" Chet edged his mount toward Brett, and now Havolin saw the spreading blotch staining the younger man's left coat sleeve; saw that the gun that had killed Prel was still clenched in Chet's right fist.

"I've taken a lot of pushing around from my father, Havolin." Chet's voice was trembling. "But I won't take any more from you — nor from anyone else." His left cheek twitched, and Brett saw the misery in the man's eyes. And he guessed at the hell this man must have lived through. Evidently Bully Armstrong's roughshod methods were not confined to outsiders.

He made a motion toward the body. "He's dead. I reckon I owe you more than the price of a cayuse, Chet —"

The Armstrong boy shrugged. "He worked for Big Diamond. But he was no good. I knew what he was heading back for, Havolin, when he left on the way to the spread." Chet took a deep breath. "My father may be all the valley folks think he is. But he'd never shoot an unarmed man, nor order one of his riders to do it. I want you to believe that, Havolin."

Brett ran his tongue over his split lips. "I believe only one thing about your paw," he said bleakly. "He's got a licking coming to him — a licking he'll never forget!"

Chet grinned wryly. "You're a stubborn fool, Havolin." Under his breath he added: "But I see what Carol meant —"

"What?"

"Nothing!" Chet snapped. He holstered his gun and indicated Prel. "Hoist him up across my saddle, Havolin. He worked for Big Diamond. Big Diamond will bury him."

Brett shrugged. Setting his teeth, he lifted the body. With Chet's right hand helping, they got Prel across Chet's saddle. A drop of bright blood, working down Chet's dangling arm, fell on the back of Brett's hand.

"Better come into town and let a doctor look at that arm," Brett suggested.

Chet shook his head. "Carol'll do a better job."

He waited until Brett walked over to Prel's cayuse and climbed into saddle. "Follow the wagon ruts until you hit the main road. Then turn left. You're five miles from town."

Havolin nodded. "I had you figured different," he said thickly. "Just goes to show, you can't tell a man by the striped company he keeps." He made a short casual gesture with his arm. "Thanks."

Chet rode past Brett, heading for the shadows ringing the clearing. He didn't even look back.

Fifteen minutes of riding brought Brett Havolin to the main road, and a short while later he picked up the lights of Benton Wells against the night. The steady jolting punished his body, and he felt light-headed under the band of pain circling his head.

He slowed the steeldust to a walk as he headed up River Road, and when he saw the sign marking Thompson's PALACE BAR he turned the steeldust to the rack and dismounted.

A half-dozen men lined the bar rail. Twice that many were scattered among the tables. Brett spotted the gambler at his table by the far wall. Thompson was sitting in a three-handed stud poker game. He was facing the door, and he saw Havolin come in, head for the bar. Thompson pushed his hand into the discards and got to his feet.

Havolin turned as Thompson touched his shoulder. He said thickly: "I've come for that drink, Mr. Thompson."

"Sure, son." The gambler indicated the far end of the bar, away from the customers turning curious faces toward them. Havolin followed him. Thompson made a quick motion to the bartender, who came immediately. He set glasses and a bottle in front of them and moved away.

Thompson poured.

The liquor burned briefly in Havolin's battered mouth. He set the glass down, eyed his bruised features in the bar mirror. He looked worse than he felt, he thought grimly. There was a yellowish-green bulge over his left eye that interfered with the movement of his eyelids. His lips were puffed to about twice their size. Dried blood stained his cheek, his chin, and spotted his jacket.

Thompson refilled his glass. "Need help, Brett?"

"No." Havolin thumbed his hat back on his red hair. His grin was lopsided. "A couple more of these under my belt and I'll amble on —"

The Palace doors swung hard, banging against the inner wall. The flow of talk ran out as men turned their

71

attention to the tall, rangy lawman shouldering his way inside.

The sheriff made a slow deliberate survey of the bar. He had an unhurried, dogged way about him that commanded respect. He saw Havolin at the end of the bar, turning to face him, and he walked across the room, skirting the silent men at the near tables.

Thompson frowned. He waited until the sheriff stopped beside him. He indicated the bottle then, made his voice affable. "On the house, Ray?"

The sheriff shook his head. "Not tonight." He looked Brett over carefully, noting the assorted bruises. A spare smile lifted the corners of his mouth.

"I saw you ride up the street on the steeldust you tied at the rack. Earlier this evening I saw Prel ride out of town on that same cayuse." His voice hardened, probed accusingly. "Now you tell me what happened, Havolin!"

"I could tell you to go to blazes!" Brett snarled. The two drinks on an empty stomach were dulling the soreness of his body.

"You could," Hogan agreed sourly. He dropped the heel of his right hand to his Colt. "And then we'd take a little walk down the street. To my office."

Havolin nodded. "Prel's dead. The steeldust is mine. If you want the answer to that, ride up to Big Diamond and ask Chet Armstrong why Havolin is riding a Big Diamond horse!"

The sheriff shook his head. "I'm asking you the questions, smart boy!"

Brett pushed away from the bar, temper flaring in his eyes. "I've taken one beating tonight, Sheriff. Don't push me!"

Hogan's weatherbeaten face darkened with a dogged anger. "I'm still askin', fella!"

Thompson stepped quickly in front of Havolin. "You're pushing that star too hard, Ray," he suggested flatly. "You got something special against Havolin?"

Hogan took in a slow breath. "I'm just doing my job," he said. There was a trace of hesitation now in his manner; he obviously didn't want to buck this man. "This pilgrim's been raisin' ructions since —"

"He's been treated like some kind of unwanted polecat since he arrived in town," the gambler snapped. "It's time someone showed him a little hospitality. I don't know how he got that cayuse. But if he says that animal belongs to him, I'm backing him, Ray!"

Hogan considered this. Thompson was a power in town — and while Ray knew some day he'd have to buck this man, he decided this was not the time or the place.

"All right, Havolin!" he muttered harshly. "I'll take that ride to Big Diamond. But if I don't get the right answers, you better be out of this town when I come looking for you!"

Havolin watched him turn, walk out of the bar. He looked at Thompson. "Thanks," he said dryly. "When I get ready to leave, you can have the Flying Club."

A glitter burst in Thompson's eyes, fading like the burst of a Roman candle against a night sky. "You leaving?"

"When I settle a few scores," Brett said. He pushed his glass away from the bartender, who was tilting the bottle again. "Before I leave, I'd like to know your reasons for wanting to buy Tony's hole-in-the-wall spread."

Thompson smiled crookedly as he turned to pour himself another drink. "It's personal, Havolin. But I'll tell you." He raised his glass and drank the whiskey in a gulp, and his face took on a subtle change as he set down the glass. His voice was bitter.

"I came to the valley a year after Frank Armstrong. I was two years married. I staked out my claim, built a one-room house, bought a hundred head. My wife had inherited some money. Armstrong was beginning to elbow his way through the valley. He was spreading out, and he decided he wanted my place. When I wouldn't sell he started to crowd me. He cut me off from water. I hung on —" His jaw tightened, and a look of hate flared in his gaze. "I hung on until the night my wife died, in childbirth." He turned and looked at Brett then, his mouth quirking. "I've hated Frank Armstrong since that day."

Brett nodded slowly. "You've got company," he muttered.

CHAPTER
SEVEN

Out on the walk, Brett suddenly didn't feel like taking the long ride back to the Flying Club. He put his shoulder to the post and looked down the dark street where men and women made shadows . . . He heard a man's quiet laughter, and it came through the night quite clearly.

He didn't belong in Benton Wells. He was an outsider, a man meddling in something all these people wanted forgotten. He had been shang-haied out of this town and beaten and set afoot and no one cared. He had the feeling that Tony Mareno had been an outsider, too . . .

He reached in his pocket and found one uncrushed cigar and lighted it with fingers that trembled slightly from weariness. But the old arrogance was in his eyes as the match flare highlighted his features and stubbornness made deep lines around his mouth.

A rider came out of an alley up the street and turned toward him and rode past. Brett followed the shadowy figure with his glance.

The sheriff was wasting no time. Hogan was riding to Big Diamond, and Brett wondered what story he would be told. If Bully Thompson wanted to frame him, there was little to hinder him. He had had trouble with Prel before, and he had come into town on Prel's horse.

All Chet Armstrong had to do would be to deny any part in tonight's happenings.

Brett considered this in the light of what had happened, and a cold chill crept down his back. Chet Armstrong was an uncertain ally. And Ray Hogan was a strange man: an honest sheriff hiding something. From the first he had shown his dislike of Havolin. Brett had the sure knowledge that Hogan was waiting only for the barest excuse to jail him.

Standing there, he felt the weight of the opposition against him. He was an intruder in this country, and Big Diamond ran it.

He threw away his cigar as the tobacco bit into the still raw cuts in his lips. He stepped down and untied the steeldust. The animal yanked back, and he hauled it around with hard hand.

He rode down the street to the looming bulk of the Trail House and left the animal at the rail. It was late enough so that the lobby was cleared of loungers.

There was no one at the desk or behind it, but a lamp, turned low, cast a dim light. He banged his palm lightly over the desk bell. On the third try a thin, gawky man appeared from a door behind the counter . . . He rubbed sleepy eyes as he came up behind the desk.

"I want a room for the night," Brett said. "I'll probably sleep late and I won't want to be disturbed."

The clerk eyed Havolin's bruised face with restrained curiosity. He nodded and reached behind him for a key. "Number ten — upstairs and way back."

Havolin picked up the key. "I have a cayuse outside. A steeldust branded Big Diamond. Have someone take it over to Baker's Livery for a rubdown, feed and a stall. Put it on my bill."

"Big Diamond?" The clerk's voice was cautiously questioning.

Brett put both hands on the edge of the counter and leaned forward. "I'm collecting horses," he said shortly. "That steeldust better be at the livery when I stop by in the morning."

He turned and went upstairs and found his room at the far end of the hall. He closed the door behind him and lighted the lamp and gazed around the room, eyeing the meager furnishings with jaundiced eyes. There was a bed, and for the moment that was all he needed.

He walked to the door, slid the bolt, turned and kicked off his boots. He lay face down across the faded counterpane and fell asleep at once.

The lamp burned out during the night . . .

Chet Armstrong rode back to Big Diamond, a hurt, bitter youngster sick with the weight of a long unresolved problem. He had stood aside these many years and watched his father run roughshod over the feelings of others — a man who put himself and Big Diamond above everything else.

He couldn't take much more of it.

Until Brett Havolin had come to Benton Wells he had believed that Tony Mareno's death had been the result of an accident. Even Carol had not suspected. His father had shrugged Tony's death off with a sneer.

"Knew that tenderfoot couldn't last . . ."

Now, as he rode through the star-hung night, he faced the ugly suspicion that his father may have had a hand in Tony's killing.

The land opened up and fell away before him now, and in the far distance he saw the lights of Big Diamond against the night shadows. Usually they had a friendly glow; Chet had known them all his life and he knew them in the darkness, shaping for him the outlines of the big house and the reach of the land to the bench beyond.

He rode through the gateway, leaning over to unfasten the leather thong which held the gate closed. He didn't bother to close it. He rode in the uncertain shadows of the straight road flanked on the south by a close-massed wind-break of tall eucalyptus trees; his nose caught the old familiar musklike smell of them and heard the slithery whispers overhead.

Ed Makin was just crossing the yard, heading for the lighted bunkhouse, when Chet rode up. The little puncher paused and eyed him with sudden interest.

Chet dismounted somewhat awkwardly. His arm was beginning to throb and he felt light-headed. He leaned wearily against the bay.

Makin came over. In the starlight his face was narrow, stiff. He put his hand on Prel's back, and his voice was quick. "Is he dead?"

Chet nodded. "Get some of the boys to help. Take him into the tool shed. We'll bury him in the morning."

Makin's quick breathing was audible in the night. "Prel said he was going to town for tobacco. What happened? He run into trouble?"

Chet nodded. He didn't feel like talking about it now. "Take care of him, Ed. He worked for Big Diamond — he's got a burial owing him."

He left the small man by the bay and walked stiffly toward the lighted ranchhouse. The cloying odor of honeysuckle came to him as he neared the vine-tangled veranda. The kitchen window was open and he could hear Carol humming a tune. The smell of freshly baked apple pie reached him as he mounted the steps.

He wondered how she'd take the news of tonight's happenings.

Frank Armstrong was reading the week-old newspaper he had picked up in his mailbox in town when Chet entered. He was sprawled heavily in his big chair under the elk antlers, his sleeves rolled up to his elbows, his boots off. A bead-fringed oil lamp cast its light into his lap.

He glanced up at Chet, grunted a greeting, and dropped his attention to the paper. Chet ignored him and headed for the kitchen. He was almost in the doorway when his father's voice halted him.

"Wait a minnit, son! What happened to you?"

Chet looked back. Frank Armstrong had dropped the paper and was staring at him, his eyes frowning under heavy brows.

"Got shot," he answered curtly. He wanted to let it go at this until he felt better. His arm was like a dead weight now, and at the edge of the numbness fiery pains were beginning to reach across his shoulder.

"Shot?" Armstrong came to his feet, a heavy, powerful man with lowered head. "Where did you go after we left the clearing?"

"I followed Prel," Chet said. He wished he could have avoided this; he wasn't sure he was up to it. He heard footsteps and Carol's face appeared in the kitchen doorway; he saw her out of the corners of his eyes.

"You have trouble with Prel?" His father's voice had held quick suspicion.

"Yeah." He took a deep breath. Carol's voice came quickly in the momentary silence. "Dad — he's hurt. Can't you see — ?"

"I want to know what happened!" Armstrong growled. "If Prel did this I'll —"

"Prel's dead!" Chet said. "I killed him!"

Armstrong stopped. He put his big head down, eyed his son from under heavy brows. He was like some bull buffalo, confused by something he couldn't quite see.

"You killed Prel? Why?"

Chet told him, flatly, without embellishment. "I had an idea why he left us," he muttered. "He didn't ride to town. He went back for Havolin . . ."

He heard Carol gasp but he went on doggedly: "Havolin could hardly stand up. And he didn't have a gun. Prel was baiting him when I rode up. He heard me and tried to kill me. I was a little luckier."

His father stood there, speechless. Chet tried to guess what was going on in his father's mind. He had expected an explosion, and there was none. For the first time in his life Chet saw his father confused.

He turned to Carol. "I need your help, sis," he said, smiling weakly. "Then I think I'll go lie down."

His father's voice came thickly across the room. "Where's Prel?"

"I brought him in," Chet answered. "The boys are laying him out in the tool shed until morning." He added quietly: "Prel worked for us. I thought we ought to bury him."

Armstrong wiped his lips with the back of a hairy hand. "Right nice of you," he growled. "What did you do with Havolin?"

"Gave him Prel's steeldust. I owed him a cayuse, for the one I shot from under him. The steeldust was a Big Diamond animal —"

Armstrong made a weary gesture, dismissing the explanation as though it didn't matter. He seemed less angry than disconcerted by this show of initiative on his son's part. He was not used to seeing Chet act on his own, and he was slow to grasp the implications of what had happened.

"I didn't tell Prel to go back for Havolin," he muttered. "You know that, don't you, son?"

Chet nodded. He turned to Carol and walked past her into the kitchen. She followed him, her face white. But she kept her silence while she helped him pull off his coat. She had to snip the sleeve off with scissors, and she cut the blood-soaked shirt away from the ugly gash.

Chet sat stoically in the chair, his arm over the basin, while she washed the wound, cleaning it with a strong antiseptic.

She asked him finally, her voice tensed. All the lightness of the day was gone out of her and there was a sick questioning look in her eyes. "What happened, Chet? I thought you and Dad rode to town for the mail. How did Brett get mixed up in this?"

Chet didn't look up at her. "He'll never change, sis." His voice was low, almost sullen. "He couldn't rest until Havolin paid for what he did to me. We went to town for the mail. But what he really wanted was Havolin. And —"

He told her about kidnaping Brett, riding him out of town; of the fight in the clearing. "It wasn't fair," he muttered. "Havolin didn't have a chance. But I don't give a tinker's damn about that. Havolin's young and tough, and in a way he's been asking for this. It's not him I'm worried about. It's Dad. He's going to find out that Havolin won't run. And then — I'm not sure what's going to happen then, sis . . ."

Carol turned away. She took bandages from a small cupboard, taking her time with them. She didn't want her brother to see her face at this moment. She had always been the strong one, the cheerful one, whenever they faced Bully Armstrong. She had sheltered Chet Armstrong from her father's outbursts, and now she saw that this had been wrong — that Chet should have been allowed to stand on his own feet. It might have been better for all of them.

She was tired of living like this. Chet was a big boy now, and her father didn't really need her. Any passable housekeeper would do better.

There was really nothing here to hold her, except a weakening loyalty. She thought of Brett and the way they had parted; her cheeks burned. What would he think of her now?

Chet guessed at some of the turmoil inside her as she bandaged his arm. "Carol — he isn't hurt bad. Banged up a little. But he'll be over it in a day or two —"

"Chet! It isn't only Brett. It's Dad. I can't help what I'm thinking about Tony . . ." Her voice shook. "I liked Tony, too. Not the same way, Chet. But now I'm remembering that Tony was killed —"

He shook his head and put his good hand on her arm. "No, sis. Whatever else he's done, Dad wouldn't do that. He didn't kill Tony. And I don't think he ordered Prel to do it."

But he wasn't sure. And the uncertainty made him feel sick inside.

Some time later Sheriff Ray Hogan rode into Big Diamond, dismounted and came to the door. He came without anger and without servility; the sheriff was his own man and he bowed neither to Frank Armstrong nor to anyone else.

Carol came to the door. Lamplight reflected from the sheriff's dusty badge; his weather-beaten face was impassive as he took his hat from his head.

"Is Chet at home, Miss Armstrong?"

Carol hesitated. She still wore the apron she had put on when she baked the pies. There was something in her face that made her seem older; she reminded Hogan of her mother.

Bully Armstrong was in the tool shed, supervising the building of a coffin for Prel, when he heard the sheriff ride into the yard. He came to the door and saw Hogan dismount and walk up the steps; he waited until the door opened and he recognized the tall, rangy figure.

He called out: "Want to see me, Sheriff?" and crossed the yard to the house with a quick, rolling stride.

Ray turned and waited for the Big Diamond cattleman to come up the steps. "I came to talk with your boy," he said. His voice was neutral. He had little liking for this big, bullying man. But he was an impersonal judge of men, too — and though he didn't like Armstrong he admired the man's energy, the push that had brought Frank Armstrong from nothing to more than comfortable wealth in twenty years.

"What for?"

"I want to ask him a few questions." The sheriff's tone was unruffled; his glance lifted to the small knot of Big Diamond men gathering in front of the tool shed.

"Ask me," the older man growled. "No need to bother Chet."

"I might — later," Ray said. His voice was cold now, a little impatient. "But I want to speak to Chet first."

Carol said swiftly: "Chet's in his room. I'll get him up —" She motioned inside. "Please come in, Sheriff."

84

"I'll wait out here, Miss Armstrong," Hogan refused politely. "What I want to ask your brother won't take much of his time."

"If it's about my foreman, Prel," Bully Armstrong chopped in bluntly, "Chet's in the clear."

Ray looked at the burly man, his eyes blank. "It's about Prel's cayuse — the steeldust. Havolin rode him into town tonight. He's got him tied up at the rack outside the Palace Bar. He claims the horse belongs to him."

Armstrong swept the air with his arm. "Forget it, Ray. The cayuse's his. Prel ain't got any use for him now —"

Chet showed up, walking toward them. His left arm was bandaged and in a sling. He had been sleeping; his eyes had a cloudy look.

"Hello, Sheriff," he greeted him. "You looking for me?"

Hogan nodded. "I just had a run-in with Havolin in town. He was riding Prel's steeldust and he looked like he'd had a hard time. When I asked him he wouldn't tell me how he got the Big Diamond cayuse. He told me to ask you."

"It's his," Chet nodded. "I gave it to him." He looked at his father, who was scowling.

"Rest of it ain't any of yore business, Ray," Armstrong snapped.

"Where is Prel?" Hogan's voice held a sharp suspicion.

"Laid out in the tool shed back there. Dead."

Hogan waited, hat in hand, but no deference in his manner. His eyes had a cold expectancy — he looked from Bully Armstrong to Chet.

Carol broke in, her voice dull. "Tell him, Dad. Tell him the whole ugly story. He has a right to know."

Frank Armstrong reddened. "Shut up and get inside!" he snapped. "A woman shouldn't stick her nose in things concerning men!"

Carol stiffened. Her face was whiter than her apron. She nodded, her voice strained, almost breaking. "I guess I deserve that. I'll go. I think I must have been waiting for this —"

She turned and walked away from them, and Chet turned to look after her, his eyes dark with growing anger. "You shouldn't have talked to her like —"

Hogan broke in with a blunt request. "I think you better tell me what happened tonight, Frank."

"It's personal!" Armstrong said brusquely. "Don't stick yore nose in what ain't any of yore business —"

"Just a minute!" Hogan snapped. "A dead man is my business."

"Is it?" Bully Armstrong sneered. "I hear that greenhorn who used to own Flying Club was killed. Don't recall you doing anything about that, Ray!"

The sheriff's eyes glittered. For a brief moment his composure was cracked; ugly temper showed in his face. Then he pulled himself together and turned to Chet, ignoring the Big Diamond boss.

"I've got no liking for Havolin," he said levelly. "He got off on the wrong foot with me when he came to town. He's too cocky for my liking. And he's a troublemaker. But murder has nothing to do with the way I feel about him. I'm asking you, Chet. What happened to your foreman. Did Havolin kill him?"

It would have been easy to pin Prel's killing on Brett, Chet saw. His father leaned against the framing, and Chet caught the gleam in his eyes, and disgust made his words bitterly curt.

"I'll tell you what happened, Ray. I killed Prel. It was me or him, and I killed him!"

"Why?" Hogan's voice was curious.

"It isn't a nice story," Chet said. "You called Havolin a troublemaker. Ever try to figure out why?"

Hogan shrugged. There was a thinning patience in his eyes.

"The day he got here I took him for a snooper around the Flying Club," Chet said grimly. "I shot his horse from under him. It wouldn't be so bad if it had stopped with that. But Prel was sent around, later, to run him off the spread. You heard what happened to Prel?"

"Shut up!" Armstrong growled. "The sheriff ain't interested in Havolin —"

"Let him talk," Hogan said softly.

"My father couldn't let it stay that way," Chet muttered. "He had to make Havolin pay for the way he'd treated Big Diamond. So tonight we kidnaped him, hogtied him and smuggled him out of town. Right under your nose, Hogan. Maybe you wouldn't have cared anyway."

"What happened?" Hogan's voice was thin.

Chet told him. "We left him there, where he dropped. But Prel rode back. I had an idea what he was up to. I followed him. When he heard me ride up he tried to kill me —"

Armstrong was shaking his head. "You fool —" he said softly.

"That's the way it was, Sheriff," Chet continued. "If Havolin was proddy when you braced him, you know why. If you want to take me in for shooting Prel, go ahead. But Havolin owns that cayuse. And he didn't kill Prel — I did!"

Hogan nodded slowly. "Reckon he's in the clear," he admitted. He made a heavy breathing sound through his nose. "I still don't like him. But the next time Big Diamond tries anything like that, on Havolin or anyone else, I'll be back, Frank. You're big in the Three Forks country. But you don't run it. Nobody is that big. Don't make me ride back this way — on law business!"

He put his hat back on his head and started to turn away. Chet said: "Want me in town tomorrow?"

Hogan nodded. "I'll want a statement from you concerning the shooting. There'll be a coroner's inquest sometime next week. I'll want you there."

He walked down the stairs to his cayuse and mounted. He didn't wave goodnight and got no wave in return.

Bully Armstrong sneered, "He's riding tall for a hundred-and-fifty-a-month lawdog. Next election I'll break him . . ."

But his voice lacked conviction.

CHAPTER
EIGHT

A thin line of sunlight slanted in between the bottom of the cracked green shade and the sill. It touched the legs of the wobbly dresser and crept up its scarred side, and the hotel room lightened perceptibly. A breeze stirred from the far reaches of the southland and flapped the shade; the frayed tassel pull beat softly against the wall below the window.

Brett heard it as he lay on the verge of wakefulness. He stirred, then rolled over on his back. He looked up at the ceiling and remembered last night. His face felt stiff, and passing his fingers over the raspy beard stubble, he encountered streaks of dried blood.

Last night came into sharp focus then; he swung around and sat on the edge of the bed and ran his fingers through his hair.

His body felt stiff and his ribs pained him when he moved. He forced himself to get up and walk to the window and let the shade up.

The sun came into the room in full flood, pointing up the dust and boot scars on the wide board floor. He looked down on a row of flat, tar-papered roofs and beyond them to the hills crinkling the horizon. It was a clear crisp day with the hazy edge of heat already graying the hills. He couldn't see the street from his window, but he heard the sound of traffic and he guessed that it was late.

He took a deep breath and a grin split his swollen lips. Heck, he had felt worse. He turned to the water pitcher and basin and splashed some water over his face and neck, washing the blood from his features. The stiffness went out of him as he moved around and his face, though still swollen in spots, had a passable appearance as he glanced at it in the mirror.

He combed his hair, placed his hat on his head at a jaunty angle, and went out.

He paused in the lobby. The ornately carved clock on the wall over the dining room arch chimed stridently; he saw that it was ten o'clock.

The dining room was deserted. He looked around him, undecided, and was about to leave when a motherly-looking woman came to the kitchen door, hands on hips, and called:

"Late, ain't you?" She was a florid-faced, gray-haired woman, built like a cracker barrel, with thick red hands. "You hungry?"

He nodded. "Enough to eat a double ration, ma'am."

"Never knew a healthy man who wasn't," she retorted. "Sit down at any of the tables an' I'll fetch you some eggs an' coffee."

He waved. "Much obliged." He walked to the table nearest the kitchen and sat down. Waiting, he heard her voice raised against the protests of someone in the kitchen. It was a man's thin voice, and hers rose above

90

it . . . "A man's hungry he oughta be fed. Quit yore grumblin' an' turn over a couple . . ."

Brett searched his pockets for a cigar. He found one only slightly damaged, lighted it. He settled back, and the thought came to him that now he would be glad to leave, after he had settled with Bully Armstrong —

He heard his name called and turned.

Lorna Marlin was in the lobby entrance, smiling at him. She waved, and he stood up and nodded and made a motion to a chair at the table. She came into the dining room just as the woman came out of the kitchen, carrying a loaded tray.

Lorna said: "How did you do it, Brett? Gladys doesn't usually feed anyone between hours."

The older woman eyed her with judicial calm. "I feed who I want, when I want," and walked away, back stiff.

Brett grinned. "I know when I'm appreciated." He pulled a chair out for Lorna. "Please join me. I like company when I have breakfast — feminine company."

Lorna hesitated. She glanced toward the lobby, shrugged. "I did want to see you," she said. She sat down, but shook her head at Brett's offer of coffee. She watched him eat, a small smile in her eyes.

"Walk into a door last night, Brett?"

Something in her voice, its lack of concern, its hint of amusement, nettled him. He looked at her somewhat coldly.

"The door had two hands," he said.

She laughed softly. "Why, Brett — you're angry!"

He let a grin come to his lips. "Reckon I was. I expected a little more sympathy from you —"

"But I am sympathetic," she countered. She reached across the table and laid a gloved hand on his arm. "Who did it, Brett?"

"Big Diamond's boss — Bully Armstrong." The smile left him and a bleak look crept into his eyes. "He didn't like the way I treated his son or his foreman, and he decided to handle it himself."

"You've had nothing but trouble since you came here," Lorna said swiftly. "Why stay? There's nothing here for you."

"Maybe I'm just stubborn," he answered. "I don't like to run with another man's prod in my back. When I leave I want to leave on my own hook. And I'm still interested in finding out who killed Tony."

"That's Ray Hogan's job," she replied, "not yours. Let Ray handle that."

He eyed her closely now. He saw only casual interest in her face, but she did not meet his glance.

"It's the sheriff's job," he admitted. "But I don't think Hogan's looking too hard for Tony's killer."

Her eyes widened now. "Why do you say that?"

"Because I think the sheriff knows who killed Tony. And he's not interested in arresting the killer."

She pulled her hand back and stood stiffly. "I think you're wrong, Brett. Ray may not be the shrewdest sheriff, but he's honest. He's nobody's hireling. Big Diamond doesn't own him. And he has no reason to cover up for anyone —"

Unless he's in love. The thought came to Brett then, unbidden and undreamed, and the full implication of this straightened him. But he didn't voice it. He studied

92

this girl across the table, seeing a tall, worldly woman with the faint lines of purpose around her mouth.

Lorna Marlin knew what she wanted out of life. And, contrary to Tony's letters, she had not wanted Tony. She had not wanted Tony because Tony was nobody, a man with little money and no future. Lorna was Mady Marlin's daughter; she had been shaped by the older woman's disappointments. Lorna Marlin would marry a rich man when she married. She might laugh and play with Tony and with Brett. But the road that would lead her to the altar would be lined with greenbacks or silver.

He saw this in her and thought of Carol Armstrong. Carol would demand something, too. But it would be a more human want. She would want a man to love her and trust her . . . and that would be enough for her.

Brett put his attention on her. She was watching him with a troubled frown.

"You had the look of a man with guilty thoughts," she said discerningly. "I hope you don't think Ray is covering up for me!"

"Why would you want to kill Tony?" he countered. "He was in love with you."

"Why, indeed!" She smiled coyly. "Please believe me, Brett — until you told me I believed that Tony's death had been an accident. I have no idea who would have wanted to kill him."

Havolin changed the subject. "You said you wanted to see me —"

"I really came looking for Ray," she said quickly. "Last night someone stole the two horses I keep in the small corral behind the house. I came to tell Ray about it. I didn't find him in his office and came to the hotel . . ."

Brett pushed his empty coffee cup aside. "I'll ride back and help you look for them."

Her eyes grew distant. "Oh, no need. You seem to have enough troubles of your own." She stood up. "I had hoped you would be in a selling mood, and that you would be willing to accept my bid." She made a small moue with her lips. "For friendship's sake?"

He didn't smile with her. "I wasn't thinking of giving the Flying Club away," he said cynically. "Perhaps if you had the money — ?"

"Oh, but I have! That is," she caught herself, "if you aren't asking all kinds of money for the place."

"I thought you and your mother were barely getting by," Brett said. He was leaned back now, studying her, and she flushed under his deliberate appraisal.

"Mother inherited a little from Father's estate," Lorna replied. Her voice was cold now; she made no effort to keep up the pretense of intimacy. "It's been in trust with Mr. Baggett at the bank. Mother didn't want to touch it except for an emergency."

"And you think this is an emergency?"

"I told you we like privacy," she said, exasperated. "Rather than have Big Diamond take it over and begin to crowd us, Mother agreed we should use that money to buy the Flying Club. Please think it over, Brett. The ranch means nothing to you. But it can mean much to us. I agree to match any offer you may receive from Frank Armstrong —"

"And Thompson?"

"Mr. Thompson, too. Although I'm surprised to hear he wants to buy the Flying Club. I can see no reason why a gambler would want to invest in a tumbledown ranch. Do you?"

"No," Brett agreed. "But I can't see why Mr. Baggett would want it, either. Yet he was one of the parties who let Kinsman know he wanted to buy the Flying Club."

"Walter's a business man," Lorna answered promptly. "Quite possibly he merely wanted the ranch, if he could get it for a very reasonable price, as a future investment. I don't believe he's serious about buying it now. Not with Big Diamond and Thompson bidding for it."

"And yourself," he reminded her.

"Yes." There was color in her cheeks. "You know why I want the ranch, Brett. Consider it as a favor to me, if you will. But I am prepared to pay you ten thousand dollars for it."

He raised an eyebrow. "I think Tony paid less than five for it. Is it worth that much to you?"

"Only because I would not want to see Armstrong as my close neighbor," she retorted. "Please consider my offer, Brett."

He nodded. "I will." He got up as she rose and stood by his chair as she left the dining room. There was a thoughtful look in his eyes as he watched her . . .

Brett settled his bill at the desk and walked out. Benton Wells was astir with morning activity. Passersby cast curious glances at the bruised-faced man on the hotel steps.

No one nodded, and he saw no one he knew. He was a stranger here, and the town was not friendly. Perhaps it was because Big Diamond had put its stamp of disapproval on him.

He reached in his pockets for a cigar and found only crumpled tobacco. He thought of Sam Morrison waiting for him in Beaumont, and he had a sudden desire to chuck it all and take the next stage out.

Still, the question of Tony's death would always nag him. He couldn't leave until he had the answer.

He walked across the street to the general store. Orrin was scooping crackers out of a barrel. A ten-year-old boy was standing by, holding a paper bag open. At the dry goods counter a matronly woman was fingering a bolt of cloth.

Brett waited until Orrin was through with the boy. The storekeeper came over, blinking at Havolin from behind his spectacles.

"Thought you had forgotten about your order," Orrin remarked testily. Then, noting the bruises on Brett's face, his tone softened. "Run into trouble?"

Brett shrugged. "Some." He didn't want to talk about it with this garrulous man. "I'll have a half-dozen cigars, those perfectos." He put five in his pocket and lighted one.

"Tony ever mention to you about finding anything valuable on his spread?" he asked casually.

Orrin was lifting Brett's sack of groceries to the counter. He shook his head. "If there had been anything of value on that spread, Phil would have found it. Phil was always looking for easy money."

Brett frowned. "Any strangers in town about the time Tony was killed?"

Orrin's eyes seemed enormously enlarged behind his lenses. He fiddled with the bag. "None I recall. You might ask at the Trail House, though. Anyone new in Benton Wells would put up at the hotel —"

Either the man knew nothing, or he was too frightened to talk. But Brett knew he'd get nothing further from the storekeeper.

"Thanks," he nodded. He settled his bill and hitched the gunny sack over his shoulder.

Crossing the street again, he headed uptown for the livery stable. The stable attendant, a wizened old man, nodded at his question. "Yep. I put the steeldust in the stall alongside yore bay. Nope — nobody came and asked about the animal."

Brett walked to the stall and looked the Big Diamond animal over. He was not an expert at judging horses, but he could see that the steeldust was a better animal than the bay. Then he remembered Lawyer Kinsman's remark that Tony's two horses, both chestnuts, were stabled here.

The hostler pointed them out. They were a matched pair and Tony had probably paid a good price for them.

Brett hesitated only briefly. He had no intention of working the Flying Club. He debated with himself whether or not he should sell the chestnuts, along with the bay he had bought from him, to Baker, the stable owner. What did a man like him need with four horses? He'd be leaving soon — and when he left he'd be riding the stage . . .

He had the hostler saddle the steeldust, gave him a half-dollar, and rode out of the barn, ducking low to avoid the overhead. He rode south along River Road and deliberately cut in to the rack in front of the sheriff's office.

Tying the steeldust at the rail, he dismounted and went inside the law office.

Ray Hogan was stretched out on a cot in the back of the narrow room, staring up at the ceiling. Something about the sheriff's face as he turned his head gave Brett a tiny shock.

There had been a deep hurt in Hogan's weather-beaten face, a dark torture in his eyes. He looked as though he had been lying there, brooding, for some time.

He got up immediately as Brett entered, a scowl wiping out all emotion from his features.

Brett said: "I thought you'd be out looking for Lorna Marlin's horses, Sheriff?"

The lawman's eyes flickered. "Something you just made up as a joke?" His voice was unfriendly, suspicious. "I'm not a hand for humor, Havolin."

"Never figgered you that way," Brett admitted easily. "Lorna stopped by the Trail House this morning. She said she was looking for you." He smiled cynically. "Reckon she didn't look in the obvious place, eh, Hogan?"

Hogan's mouth was a hard, bleak slash. "I just got in." He came over to Brett and glanced through the open door at the saddled horse tied up at the rail.

Brett said: "I'm still riding Prel's cayuse. You satisfied?"

Hogan nodded slowly. "I'm satisfied." He started to turn away, then looked back at Brett.

"Big Diamond's made a lot of mistakes," he said coldly. "Frank Armstrong ain't liked by many in the valley. In a way it's been rough on his son an' his daughter. But he didn't kill Tony. He didn't like him — Frank Armstrong ain't the kind to take to anyone right off. But he let Tony alone. And he'd leave you alone, if he thought you wasn't goin' to give him trouble."

"It's a bit late for that, Sheriff," Brett growled.

Hogan pointed a finger at Brett, his voice roughening. "Maybe Frank was right, then!" he snapped. "He said Thompson was behind his troubles. He claimed you and Tony are only fronts for Thompson —"

"Armstrong's got a guilty conscience," Brett jeered. "I never saw Thompson, or knew of him, until I came to Benton Wells."

"You and he seem to hit it off right well," Hogan snarled. "What's between you and that tinhorn gambler?"

"Nothing, except that Thompson's the only man in town who's acted like I was human!" Brett's eyes had a bleak, bitter look. "He gave me a helping hand when you and Big Diamond tried to run me out of the country. He wants to buy the Flying Club, too. And he has a darn good reason why. Maybe that's why I'll sell to Thompson. When I decide to leave, Hogan."

The sheriff shrugged. "That's yore privilege. But Frank Armstrong won't like it —"

"It touches me," Brett snapped, "right here . . ."

He turned his back on the scowling sheriff and walked out. Hogan came to the door. He waited until Brett had mounted and swung away from the rack, heading for the trail out of town. He was still in the doorway when he saw Lorna Marlin leave the bank.

He watched her with eyes suddenly turned soft; the hardness was gone from his crumpled face. He turned and slammed his hat down on the cot . . .

CHAPTER
NINE

It was late afternoon when Brett Havolin rode into the Flying Club yard. The ride had not put him in a cheerful frame of mind. He had the dismal feeling he'd never find out who had killed Tony. He couldn't even get anyone except Kinsman to admit that Tony had been killed.

Ray Hogan's actions puzzled him. The sheriff disliked him because Lorna Marlin had played up to him. But Brett felt that was only a partial explanation for the man's hostility. The sheriff wanted him out of the valley. Was it because he didn't want anyone pushing the problem of Tony's killing?

It seemed like that to Havolin. And if Hogan was covering up for someone, it was Lorna.

Brett considered this possibility now, finding it not to his liking, either. Why would Lorna have wanted to kill Tony? Perhaps because she wanted the Flying Club. Still, he couldn't believe this girl could cold-bloodedly shoot anyone . . .

Hogan knew. But his hands were tied because he loved Lorna Marlin. Suddenly Brett felt tired of it all. Tony had been a fool to think he could change his life overnight, come out here as a stranger and sink his roots. He was no cattleman. Oil was his business — he should have stuck to it.

He knew he was arguing this to convince himself, not Tony.

"You're a cockeyed fool," he told himself. "You laughed at Tony for coming out here and thinking he could settle down. Don't fall for the same sort of claptrap."

He stripped the steeldust of its saddle and turned it loose in the shed, tying it to the crib bars. Then he walked out, carrying the sack of groceries.

The sun was a huge ball of fire on the horizon. Its light came in through the door, reddening the floor boards. Brett looked around, half hoping to see the slim figure of Carol Armstrong by the stove. But there was no one in the cabin.

He dropped the groceries on the table, took the coffee pot and went out for water. He got a fire started in the stove and cooked beans and bacon. It was dark when he sat down at the table to eat. He didn't light a lamp. He kept the door open and looked across the darkening yard to the stars. A coyote made a dark skulking shadow by the barn, and from somewhere inside the rooster crowed his uneasy challenge.

Brett got up and walked to the door, and the coyote melted away. The rooster crowed again and settled down to sleep.

Brett stood in the doorway a long time, watching the moon come up . . .

The rooster, crowing lustily, wakened him next morning. He got up and walked to the battered dresser

102

and looked in the fogged mirror. Most of the swelling had disappeared, but his face held a variety of bluish-yellow marks that made an incongruous pattern. He hadn't looked this bad since the night he and Tony had gotten into a free-swinging fight with a half-dozen muckers from a rival well in Beaumont's Red Emporium.

He wagged a finger at his image in the mirror. "Time you settled down, fella," he chided. "You only got so much wear and tear coming to you. Remember, you ain't twenty any more —"

He walked out into the kitchen in his stocking feet and surveyed the empty woodbox behind the stove. His dirty dishes lay on the table where he had left them last night. Sunlight made a cheerful pattern in the room, and somehow this morning his spirits were high. He walked to the door, flung it open, and took in a deep breath.

The frayed lengths of a rope that had once been a child's swing hung from a thick branch of the big pecan tree. Tony's voice came back to him: "Buy me a small spread, get married, raise some kids . . ."

Brett turned away, his mouth hardening. He walked into the bedroom, got into his boots, picked up his hat and returned to the kitchen. The fire had long since died out. He went out for some wood from the small rick against the shed and started a fire and went out again for water.

Last night's coffee was heating as he started to shave. He was hungry, but not hungry enough to want to cook his own breakfast. He sat down and drank of the bitter brew, which had not improved by staying overnight in the pot.

Cigars were a habit with him. He needed one now. He got up and went into the bedroom and felt in the pocket of the jacket on the hook behind the door. He felt paper crinkle under his searching fingers. Frowning, he drew out the letter.

It was tobacco-soiled and badly crumpled, but it was still sealed and it was addressed to him. For a moment Brett eyed it with a blank stare. Then it came to him that this was Tony's brush jacket . . . His own was on the chair beside the bed.

It looked as if Tony had written this letter to him and put it in his jacket pocket to mail it, and forgotten it.

Brett opened it.

A single sheet of paper, written on both sides in pencil. Tony had never been much of a letter writer, he remembered. He was as laconic on paper as he was voluble in conversation. But his last paragraph jarred Brett.

"*Ran across something that's got me pretty excited. Oil! Can you beat it, Brett? I left Beaumont to get away from rigs and guys like you. I wanted a piece of land I could farm, to raise some beef. And today I find an oil scout on my property. I did a little snooping and found out he's from Consolidated. He's keeping his survey quiet. But I got a hunch he's making out a copy of his report for Walter Baggett at the bank. What do you think of that? Maybe I'm sitting on a pool of oil and I don't know it. Me, an old oil man! What a laugh if it should pan out that way.*

Brett, when are you coming out here? I won a bet, remember . . ."

Brett chewed on his cigar. He thought bleakly: *You didn't have time to laugh, did you, Tony? Someone found out you knew, and killed you!*

Who?

Walter Baggett, probably. But Bully Armstrong may have found out, too. And so might Jack Thompson. So might any of the people who seemed so willing to buy the Flying Club.

He was chewing on this when he heard the rider come up to the door. For a brief moment he considered that it might be Carol. He got up and walked to the door, shoving the letter into his pocket as he crossed the room.

He flung the door open and stepped out — and looked into the cold muzzle of Chet Armstrong's Colt!

Armstrong's left arm was in a cloth sling. He held his restive mount in place with the pressure of his knees. His face was pale . . . He searched the yard and Brett and behind Brett with quick, narrowed gaze.

"Where is she?" His voice held a curious thickness.

"Who?"

"Carol." Chet edged the bay slightly around so that the sun was against his back. "She left home. I thought she might have come here."

Brett eased his weight against the framing. "What led you to think she'd be here?" he asked coldly.

"She's not home," Chet said angrily. "She came here before —"

"So you figgered she'd come here again?" Brett eyed Chet with bleak contempt. "You must have a pretty poor opinion of your sister, fella."

"I know sis!" Chet snarled. "When she found out what Dad did to you the other night, she and Dad had it out. She packed up yesterday and left —"

"She should have left Big Diamond long ago," Brett cut in thinly. "It must have been awful for her, living with that bullheaded, blind tyrant —"

Chet's Colt muzzle jerked and his pale face grew paler. "Just a minute, Brett. You've got reason not to like my father. But I'm not going to sit here an' listen to you talk like that about him." There was a strange torment in Chet's eyes. "Most people hear only the bad side of Bully Armstrong. Sure — he's like a muley steer. When he wants to do something he just puts his head down and does it. He's stepped on a lot of toes, made a lot of enemies. But he's done good for this country, too. Big Diamond's trade supports half of Benton Wells. It's Big Diamond money that built the schoolhouse. Dad was the first to put up money for a teacher, too."

Brett made a small gesture. "You came here to tell me that, Chet? Just to tell me how nice your dad is?"

"I came to find Carol!" Chet snapped. "I want her to come back home. If she was here I was going to step off this cayuse and give you the same kind of licking you got from Dad. Even with one hand I could do that, Brett!"

Havolin looked the angry youngster over. Chet was big enough, and he was mad enough, to try it. He felt a grudging respect for this confused and bitter son of Bully Armstrong.

"She's not here!" he stated flatly. "I haven't seen your sister since the day she dropped by, just to be friendly, and Prel and his boys tried to make something nasty out of it." He knew this was not exactly true. Carol had come by later, to apologize for Prel and her father. But he didn't think he ought to tell Chet Armstrong this.

Chet's Colt muzzle dropped. "I'll take your word for it. I didn't really expect to find her here. But I came to tell you something, Havolin — I want to warn you. Don't think that because of what happened the other night I like you. I did it for my father. If Prel had killed you, my father would have been blamed — and he's bucking enough trouble as it is." He leaned forward over his saddle horn. "And it's Carol I'm thinking about, too. She's just mad enough at Dad, and unhappy enough, to make a move she would regret the rest of her life." His tone harshened, cutting Brett's incipient protest. "I don't know you, fella. But I know sis. She likes you. And she thinks you got a raw deal from Dad. She might just be in the mood to try to make it up to you. An unscrupulous hombre could —"

He let the implication lie between them; his eyes were dark with feeling.

Brett put it into cold words. "Might just take advantage of her? That what you driving at?"

"Thanks for putting it so nicely," Chet snarled.

"And you wouldn't want that?"

"I don't want to see sis make a fool of herself! I don't think you're the kind who belongs out here, Havolin!

Not on a two-by-four spread, raising chickens and a few mangy head of cattle. You don't sound like that kind of hombre to me! And sis wouldn't be happy with any other kind!"

Maybe this was on the level, Brett thought — but he had another idea. "You make a lot of noise, Chet. I am reminded of something I read in a book once — 'Gadzooks, the man doth protest too much!' I smell a polecat. It couldn't just be that this is a roundabout way of shoving your sister at me —"

He flinched at the report, the flash and smoke and the simultaneous ripping of wood in the framing an inch from his shoulder.

He stiffened, his eyes angry . . . waiting.

Chet said: "I shot to miss that time, Brett." His voice shook with his effort to keep it even. "Don't try me again!"

"To heck with you!" Havolin snarled. "Shoot and be damned! But I'll have my say! It couldn't be that your father knows there's oil on this land?" He measured the dark look on Chet's face; he saw nothing there but narrow-eyed suspicion.

"Several people have tried to buy the Flying Club since I've taken it over," Brett said. "Your father, I understand, was one of the bidders. Why? Just because he wants a few more acres of range? Don't make me laugh! He wants the Flying Club because he found out about the Consolidated Oil's scout report on oil formation and proposed leasing. Maybe he found out the day Tony died. That is the first and only logical explanation of why Tony was found in Piute Creek with a rifle slug in him!"

Chet shook his head. "Oil? You're crazy, Havolin!"

Brett took the letter from his pocket, waved it at the rider. "Not crazy, Chet. I just found out the truth. And you can tell your father his scheme isn't going to work. He can't buy me out; he can't run me out — and he can't get his daughter to —"

Chet's gun hammer clicked back ominously. "You've got a big mouth, Havolin!" he said bleakly. "I didn't know about the oil survey and I don't think Dad did. I know Carol doesn't. And if you bother her, Havolin, I promise you I'll come after you. So help me, I'll kill you!"

He backed his cayuse away until he was out of easy gun range, then whirled and set it for the road to town at a hard run.

Havolin relaxed back against the scarred framing. He touched his cheek where a splinter had brought a smear of blood. "Guess the kid wasn't fooling," he murmured. "And I reckon he didn't know about the oil, at that."

Which didn't rule out the possibility that Bully Armstrong had known, and had taken care of Tony himself. Maybe the old cattle baron had some good in him, as his son had said. But Havolin had found little of it in his dealings with the man, or with the men he hired.

He wondered if Carol was in town, or had left the Three Forks country altogether. He thought of this, and suddenly he knew he had to see her again.

Prodded, and still hurt from the beating he had taken from Frank Armstrong, he reacted to Chet from anger and suspicion.

He had made a mistake in implying that Carol Armstrong's friendship had been nothing more than a scheme to get him to sell out to Big Diamond — he knew it now and felt the twinges of a vast self-disgust.

"Maybe I have been a little hard to get along with myself," he reflected, and he had the understanding to sneer at himself for it.

Carol would hardly be coming here again, he thought soberly — the days of easy sociability were gone. He remembered the look in her eyes when she had said she was tired of being known as Bully Armstrong's daughter.

Chet was probably right in being concerned for her. In her present defiant mood, Carol Armstrong might readily take a step she would be sorry for later.

Too restless to stay around the ranch, Brett Havolin saddled the steeldust immediately after he had cooked his breakfast and rode out. He headed for the creek with the vague notion of riding to the Marlin place and sounding them out on the matter of oil on Flying Club land.

He was no geologist, but he had worked around rigs and with oil men too long not to have some idea of oil formations. And it occurred to him that if the Consolidated scout had reasons to believe there was oil under the Flying Club acres, then it was more than probable that the field extended under Marlin property.

110

There was even good reason, he speculated wryly, to believe that oil might be found under some of Big Diamond's acreage.

He came up to the high ground from which he could look across the creek to the far huddle of the Marlin buildings. He sat saddle and waited, no longer sure he wanted to break in on the Marlins this way.

Lorna Marlin was an opportunist; he flushed at the thought she must have known all along about the oil. He had little doubt now that the incident by the creek had been calculated with this in mind. It explained her offer of twice what Tony had paid for the ranch.

But however Lorna was implicated in this ugly business, Mady Marlin was innocent. She was a wisp of a woman who lived in a dream world of make-believe — he didn't want to hurt her.

He turned the steeldust away, and in the distance, just moving into the trees fringing the lower end of Piute Creek, he saw the sheriff. He couldn't mistake the set of those shoulders, the rangy body . . .

He touched heels to the steeldust and followed. He rode without hurry, and it was a half-hour later that he broke through the thin screen of cottonwoods and came upon the lawman.

The sheriff had dismounted and climbed out on a ledge of rock jutting ten feet over the rushing water. He was hunkered down, his back to Havolin, like a man searching for something upstream.

He turned and straightened immediately as he heard Brett approach.

Brett remained in saddle. "Howdy, Sheriff." His voice was cool. "This where Tony's body was found?"

It was a shrewd guess, but he saw the sheriff flinch and knew he had scored.

"Might be," Hogan admitted. "What brings you here?"

"Saw you ride this way," Brett answered. "Decided I'd like to have a talk with you."

"I've no time for small talk," Hogan said. He walked to his ground-reined cayuse a few paces downstream.

"This might change your mind," Brett growled, intercepting him. He leaned down and held out Tony's crumpled letter.

The sheriff took it, his eyes narrowing. He stepped back and read it, a frown starting in his eyes and spreading swiftly across his face.

"Tony wrote that to me," Brett said. "He never mailed it. I found it this morning in the pocket of one of his old jackets."

"Oil?" Hogan's voice held a deep surprise.

"Yeah, oil. It explains why Tony was killed, doesn't it, Sheriff?"

Hogan didn't answer. He folded the letter, replaced it in its envelope, handed it back to Brett.

"You can question Walter Baggett," Havolin pointed out. "He might lie. But I doubt he will. He's smart enough to know that a letter from your office to Consolidated will back up Tony. I'm not saying he killed him. But someone did, Sheriff. It could be Walter Baggett, or Armstrong — even Thompson."

"It could be anyone," Hogan said thickly. He reached up and tapped the star on his coat. "But that's my job,

112

remember? If Baggett or Armstrong had anything to do with Tony's killing, I'll find out. But you keep out of it, Havolin!"

"You had six weeks to find out who killed Tony!" Brett snapped. "You didn't even find out why!"

"Don't be too sure it was because of oil!" Hogan flung out harshly.

Brett paused. Something in the sheriff's stiff-necked attitude indicated the man knew much more than he was letting on. Brett had sensed this before.

"You know any other good reasons?" Hogan shrugged. He was in control of himself now; his eyes held nothing but cold unfriendliness. "That's my job and my responsibility. And you'd be a whole lot smarter if you turned things over to your lawyer to handle and got out of the valley!"

Brett leaned forward on his saddle. "So far, Hogan, I've done nothing but listen to you talk. I didn't come to town looking for trouble. I was ready to sell and clear out when Bully Armstrong kidnaped me, drove me out of town, and gave me a licking. I get mulish when someone prods me, Sheriff. You haven't got enough authority behind that tin badge to run me out of this country — and there ain't enough men on Big Diamond to do it!"

"A mule's got his points," the sheriff agreed with quiet levity. "But he's still second cousin to a jackass."

Brett suddenly grinned. He had not expected this much wit from the red-necked lawman, and he nodded now, conceding the point.

"You got relatives like that, too." He smiled. "I'll make you a promise. I'll leave the job of finding Tony's killer to you. But I've got a score to settle with Bully Armstrong that's my own. When I do I'll be ready to sell out and leave the valley."

He eased back, waved briefly, and swung the steeldust away. Hogan watched him disappear among the trees.

Oil! He sighed deeply. Maybe that was the reason for Tony's killing. But it did not lighten his burden, or rid him of the nagging torment he lived with. He fashioned a cigarette and squatted down and eyed the rushing water, his thoughts following the creek upstream . . .

CHAPTER
TEN

Carol Armstrong walked away from her brother. "No, Chet." Her voice sounded tired. "I'll not come back with you. Not now. Maybe I'll never go back." She turned by the piano. She seemed older to her brother — more possessed, and without the lightness he had always associated with his sister. He didn't like the change.

"I want to be left alone for a while," she said. "I want a chance to think this thing out."

They were in Martha Crosby's home in Benton Wells, in her front room. Carol had come here after leaving Big Diamond. Lisa Crosby was Carol's closest friend, and Chet had guessed, after checking at the Flying Club, that Carol would have come here.

Martha Crosby and her daughter, Lisa, had discreetly withdrawn, leaving brother and sister alone.

Chet took a deep breath. "He needs you, Carol. He's too bullheaded to admit it, but he needs you. More than he needs me."

She shook her head. "He doesn't really need anyone, Chet. He likes to have us around, so he can bully us, the way he's bullied everyone he has dealings with. That's all he knows. Obey his whims, or suffer the consequences. I'm tired of it, Chet. Tired of standing strong all the time." Her voice fell to a whisper. "Chet — sometimes I need help, too. Sometimes I'm weak — I need someone to lean on. I need someone who understands —"

Chet's face burned. "I think I know, sis. I haven't helped you. I'm big — bigger'n most men in the valley. But I've always felt small beside Dad. I wanted to measure up to him, and whenever I tried I failed." His voice was miserable. "He's like a rock — it's there, immovable and unyielding. When I was a boy I used to feel his arm . . . I was proud of his muscle. But I found out something, Carol. He's like all of us. He's tired, too. Under that rock he's tired. He needs someone to lean on, too. I think he's always wanted to be able to lean somewhat on me. I failed him. He built Big Diamond with that bullheaded, be-damned-to-you way of his — that's all he knows. But he'd be willing to sit back and try to be human now, if he felt someone could take over his job."

Carol shrugged. "You've tried. He never let you."

"I didn't try hard enough," her brother replied. "I was afraid. I had to kill a man to find out something about myself. I didn't enjoy killing Prel. But I found out that Dad's attitude toward me changed. And I don't feel small any more. I won't put up with his blustering threats, and he knows it now. He's confused. Right now he's back home, waiting for you to come back and say you're sorry. If it's only a question of pride, Carol — ?"

116

She shook her head. "I'll think about it, Chet. But I won't come back with you. Not today."

He made a small relieved gesture. "I want you back, too, sis. I need you. Not to fight my battles any more. But the ranch is gloomy without you. It isn't home —"

She didn't say anything, and after a moment he turned and went to the door. Then he looked back at her, his face settling into a faint frown. "I stopped by Havolin's place, sis. I — I —" He flushed, hating to say it.

Carol stiffened, a faint horror coming into her eyes. "You thought that I — ?"

He nodded. "I reckon I made a fool of myself," he muttered. "Havolin as much as told me so. But I didn't want you to —" He fumbled and lost his voice under her blazing eyes.

"Oh, no, Chet! You let Brett think that I would run to him, like a common —"

"I know how you feel about him," Chet said. His voice was defensive. "After hearing what Dad did to him I had a crazy idea you might have ridden to him —"

Her shoulders slumped; she sagged back against the piano. A small smile touched her lips. "I might have. Perhaps I should have. But I still have my pride left, Chet. It may be all that I have left — but I still have that. You're right about the way I feel about him. I guessed I showed it pretty openly. I was never one to hide the way I felt. But you should have known me better than that, Chet — should have had more faith in me."

Chet stood with his back against the door. "I'm sorry, sis. I'll never be that kind of a fool again."

She didn't answer, and he saw the gleam of tears in her eyes. He cursed himself with bitter, silent reproof.

"Sis — I'll see you again? At the dance Saturday?"

Her head nodded slightly. He jammed his hat on his head and went out, closing the door firmly behind him.

Brett Havolin arrived in Benton Wells in the afternoon. He tied up at the bank and went inside and waited in line. There were two other people in front of him, one depositing money and the other withdrawing. When they had gone he slid his pass book under the grille and asked to withdraw two hundred dollars.

The clerk made the proper entries, counted out the cash. He studied Brett's bruised face, but offered no comment.

Stuffing the money in his pocket, Brett asked to see Mr. Baggett.

"He's not in," the clerk said. "Mr. Baggett left this morning for Rawlins. He'll be back Saturday."

Brett considered this. He had wanted to show the banker Tony's letter and watch him try to explain it. But it looked as if he would have to wait until Saturday. Two more days. Then he remembered that the Big Diamond shindig was this Saturday, too, and a smile touched his lips.

It looked as though Saturday was going to be a big day.

He left the bank and stood on the walk, and then an idea came to him. He mounted and rode around the corner of Coyote Street and went into the Dusty Hole.

The bartender shook his head. "He was here less than an hour ago. You check his office?"

Brett shook his head. He went out and rode to Lawyer Kinsman's office and went up the narrow, shaky stairs.

He found the attorney asleep in a chair, a volume of *Harper's Weekly* by his side, an empty bottle of Harper's whiskey on the window shelf close at hand.

Brett shook him awake.

He put a ten-dollar bill under Kinsman's bulbous nose, and when the lawyer's bleary eyes focused on it he said sharply: "I've got a job for you. I'm ready to sell the Flying Club."

Kinsman brushed Brett's hand away. He came to his feet and started dusting his clothes. Then he looked Brett over, mustering a false dignity. "Someone worked you over, eh? Finally pounded some sense into you, I see."

He turned for the bottle on the window sill, scowled when he saw it was empty. "Reckon I'd better take that," he nodded, plucking the bill from Brett's fingers.

He tucked it expertly in his vest pocket. "Who are you selling to?"

"First man — or woman — who meets my price," Brett answered.

Kinsman blinked. "That won't be too hard —" He thrust his face out belligerently. "What are you asking?"

"Fifty thousand dollars!"

Kinsman made a sarcastic sound with his lips. "You're crazy! Your friend, Tony, paid less than five thousand for the Flying Club — and most folks around here figured Phil robbed him."

Brett grinned. "Maybe Tony wasn't the fool most folks around here figured." He jabbed a forefinger against Kinsman's stomach. "You've been advising me to sell. That's my price. And there's a thousand dollar commission in it for you —"

Kinsman threw up his hands. "I'll tell them what you're asking. But I think something was knocked loose up there —" He tapped the side of his head indicatively.

"I think you'll find my price is going to knock quite a few things loose around here, Mr. Kinsman," Brett said gravely. "Just be sure Mr. Baggett gets the word. He's out of town right now — I checked at the bank. But he's expected back Saturday."

Kinsman nodded. "I'll tell him." He held out his hand, palm up. "You owe me ninety dollars more, son. You've finally taken my advice."

"You'll have a thousand when you close the deal with a buyer," Brett pointed out.

"I'm a practical man," Kinsman snapped. "A hundred in my hand is worth —"

"A thousand you might never get," Brett finished. He dug in his pocket and added the rest of the fee. "It'll come out of your commission," he stated pleasantly.

"If there ever is a commission!" Kinsman growled. "I still think you're crazy to think anyone will even consider that tumbledown spread at — eh, wait a minute!" His eyes narrowed on Brett's smiling face. "You've got something up your sleeve?"

"In my pocket," Brett corrected. "Don't get drunk before you've earned that hundred. I want Armstrong notified, too."

He left then, pleased with himself. He had an idea that a lot of things were going to change, once Kinsman got the word around.

He paused on the corner of Coyote Street and River Road. He had time on his hands, and he was at loose ends. He considered dropping by the Palace Bar and having a talk with Thompson. The gambler was the only seemingly honest man in town. The man hated Armstrong, with good reason. But he had never pushed Brett about the Flying Club — rather, he had helped him when help was most needed.

He saw Carol Armstrong then, coming up the street on the opposite plank walk. She was with a girl her own age, a slightly heavier girl with quick, pealing laughter.

Crossing the street, Brett intercepted them in front of Cosgrove's Pharmacy.

"Hello," he said, taking his hat from his head. He was smiling, but it was not a cocksure smile — he felt humble in front of this girl.

Carol nodded her greeting. She searched his face, looking for his reaction to her brother's visit. But he seemed glad to see her, and there was neither unfriendliness nor mockery in his eyes. He seemed serious, which was a change from the way she remembered him. She looked at the discolored bruises on his face and remembered how they had happened.

She said in a small voice: "Good afternoon. Lisa — this is Mr. Havolin."

The Crosby girl looked Brett over with unabashed interest. Carol had not told her too much about this man, but she had heard gossip.

"You're not as handsome as Tony," she said bluntly. "And from what I hear, much more quarrelsome." She smiled, and her light gray eyes were teasing. "But Carol should have told me more about you."

He took her proffered hand. "You obviously didn't know Tony as well as I did." He grinned. "And I really look much better than you see me now."

Lisa laughed. "I like a man with a sense of humor," she said.

"And I'd like to talk with Carol."

Carol stiffened. "Really, Mr. Havolin — I have nothing to —"

"Oh, talk with him," Lisa urged. "I've got to get Mother's headache powders and a few other things. I'll see you back at the house."

She nodded briskly at Havolin. "Be kind to her, sir." And she flounced into the pharmacy.

Carol said: "I really am no longer interested in your problems, Mr. Havolin —" She paused as two older women with market baskets in hand came by.

Brett took her arm. "This is no place to talk. And you look a little pale. A walk in the sun will do you good. I know a place on the bluffs —"

She hesitated.

"I want to apologize," he said quickly. "I'd rather do it in private."

She went with him then. They headed for the creek and the bluffs and found a quiet spot over the placid

122

flow of water below. The town was less than five hundred yards behind them, but trees screened them from view. Somewhere farther down they could hear splashing and the laughter and whoops of boys, but the play was distant enough not to intrude.

She stopped. An oak grew close to the edge of the bluff, and she rested her back against it. The sun sparkled on the water below, but there was no sparkle in her eyes.

He looked at her. He had never been at a loss for words with girls before. Now he didn't know what to say. He wasn't confused, but he wanted to tell her how he felt without making it sound false. He wanted to tell her without bringing in Chet's visit this morning; she had been hurt enough.

"I told the sheriff that only one person, Jack Thompson, had treated me like a human being since I came here," he said slowly. "I was wrong. You were the first to be neighborly — to be friendly. But I was a fool." There was no pleading in his voice, only firmness, and it carried more weight because of it.

"I'm a smart guy, Carol — I know all the angles. Everyone in this world wants something for himself. That's the way I've always had things figured. Nobody does anything for anyone without thinking of what he'll get back. Some people use the velvet glove — some, like your father, the back of their hands. But it all amounts to the same thing. They want something, and that's the way they think they'll get it. So when you came along —"

"I wanted something too," she said quickly. "Something more than material gain, perhaps. We all do want something, don't we? I wanted to be friends, that's all. But I wanted that for a selfish reason, too. I wanted to be friends with you because so few of our neighbors are friendly to Big Diamond."

"I believe it now, Carol," he said. "And I want to apologize. Your father sending Prel after you didn't help. But I should have trusted you."

She smiled. It brightened her face, took the faint lines from around her mouth. "Chet told me he called on you this morning. I'm glad you didn't mention it. He's growing up, Brett — forgive him. He's getting protective now."

"I owe him my life," Brett said.

She took his arm. "Yesterday I left home. I couldn't stand it any more. Since Mother died I've had to stand up for Chet, take the brunt of my father's bad temper. He'll never change. I know that now. He'll get more irascible, like a shaggy old bear, with the years. But his growl will mean less. Chet has found that out for himself."

Brett shrugged. "I hope you're right, Carol. But he should be taught a lesson —"

Her fingers tightened on his arm. "I don't want to hurt him any more, Brett. He's back there on Big Diamond, alone. The ranch runs itself these days. He really hasn't anything to expend his energy on, so he takes it out on —"

"On Tony?"

124

Her eyes widened abruptly; she pulled her hand away and stepped back. The hurt in her eyes was deeper because of her own guilty suspicions. "Brett, you don't really believe Dad killed Tony?"

He handed her Tony's letter and waited while she read it through. She looked up at him, her eyes clouded. "But — why Dad? Tony mentions Walter Baggett —"

"Baggett doesn't seem the type," Brett muttered. "Besides, the day Tony was shot Baggett was in his office, at the bank. The sheriff verified this."

She shook her head. "My father doesn't know about this oil report," she said. "I'm sure of it. If not Baggett, then someone else —"

"It could be any of a number of other people," he agreed. "It could be the gambler Thompson. He's wanted the ranch. But I don't think he knows about this oil scout. He told me he wanted it because he hates your father —"

Carol made a quick gesture. "Many people do."

"I was ready to sell out to Thompson," he told her, "before I found this letter. He's been the only man to give me a hand when I needed it."

He told her of the backing he had received from the gambler the night the sheriff came looking for him. And he told her the story Thompson had told him, about why he hated Frank Armstrong.

"He told you that?" Carol's tone was bewildered. "Why, Thompson has never owned a ranch in the valley. He's always been what he is now — a gambler. He came into Benton Wells years ago, it's true — when I was a little girl. I know the common gossip. He came to town and bought into a partnership at the Palace Bar with Harry Clayton, and later he bought Clayton out. In the following years he's seemed to have made quite a bit of money, bought other properties —"

"Then why the enmity between him and your father?"

"I never found out all the reasons behind it," she said. "It had something to do with attentions he tried to force on Mother, years ago. I don't really know much about it. Dad never talks of it."

Brett knuckled his jaw thoughtfully. "Why would Thompson tell me that story, Carol?"

"I don't know. But he's never owned a ranch, and, as far as I know, he has never been married. You can verify that by asking anyone who's been in town long enough to know."

Brett turned and looked toward the town screened by the trees. His voice held a thin, mocking irony. "Reckon I can scratch Thompson off, too . . ." He tore a small twig and threw it over the bank in a quick gesture of disgust.

"What are you going to do now?"

"Wait." His voice was flat. "Just wait and see what happens." He took her arm. "I think I'll stay in town tonight. I haven't had a chance to repay you — for making coffee that day. Would you have dinner with me?"

She looked into his face. "Yes," she said softly, "yes . . ."

He left her at the gate in front of the Crosby cottage and walked back to River Road. The same clerk was at the desk when he asked for a room at the Trail House.

126

"Same room?" he asked, and at Brett's nod he handed Havolin the key. Brett was turning away when the clerk said apologetically: "Oh, Mr. Havolin! Almost slipped my mind. I have a telegram for you."

He reached behind him in a pigeonhole and took out the message. Havolin read it as he went up to his room. It was from Sam Morrison:

Clyde Bass anxious to throw in with us.
What shall I tell him? Waiting.

Brett crumpled the message in his fist. The irony of it struck him as he remembered Tony. Mareno had wanted only to settle down somewhere, farm a little, raise a few head of cattle, marry. Tony had come from farming folks back in Pennsylvania, and the years of kicking around the oil fields in east Texas had finally soured him.

He had come here to settle down as his ancestors had in Pennsylvania, only to find himself sitting on what could well be an underground lake of oil. It was oil which had killed Tony after all.

Brett tossed the telegram on the bed and peeled off his jacket and shirt. Even as early as this morning he had been sure he would be leaving Benton Wells after the Big Diamond shindig. Now, he wasn't sure of anything. He wasn't anxious to get back to the old life of hard work and painted women . . . in a way he had outgrown it.

He washed and noticed that his hair was getting shaggy and that he had forgotten to shave this morning.

He got back into his clothes and went out looking for a barber.

It was six o'clock when he called at the Crosby home for Carol Armstrong.

They ate in Polly's.

Looking back afterward, Brett knew it had been one of the best evenings he had ever spent. They didn't talk of Big Diamond or the Flying Club. Brett found himself talking of his boyhood in St. Louis; of his four older brothers and two sisters, and a widowed mother who had maintained a cheerfulness that wore off on her children.

His two sisters were married . . . His older brother, Jonas, had been killed at Bull Run. Elias was a doctor, and Hiram, starting as an iceman, had his own business.

He had been more fiddle-footed; he had left home at sixteen, drifted up the Missouri as a deck hand, later as a cowhand, and then down to Texas after a cattle drive to the rail town of Caldwell. Big Spindle had just blown in . . . and he was twenty. He had lived the next years with oil.

And he told Carol about Tony, and his bet with Tony.

"He liked it here," Carol said. The flickering candlelight between them softened her face; there was an appeal to her that Brett felt strongly.

"I didn't know Tony as well as you did, Brett — but I know he liked it here. He told me often he didn't regret leaving Beaumont — didn't like the life he had led there. He was a green hand at raising cattle, and I tried to help. I was brought up on Big Diamond. But

128

Tony surprised me with his knowledge of farming. He had a garden patch behind the barn, and he had plans for alfalfa along the southwest corner, near the creek . . ."

Brett nodded. "I reckon it comes to most men," he said quietly: "the feeling that time's wasting, that the days are slipping by. A man gets afraid then. I think I know now how Tony felt. One day a man gets up and looks in the mirror, and he's almost thirty, and he's afraid. There's his hat on the bedpost and a suit hanging up in the closet and he's got a big head from last night's poker session. And suddenly he sees that's all he has and all he will ever have. And he's afraid. It's a deep instinct, Carol . . . a man is only half a man when he walks alone."

She smiled. "A woman knows that sooner — she knows from the day she becomes a woman."

"It took me twenty-nine years," Brett said. "I don't regret them. I had a good time. But I feel like Tony. I never thought I'd say this, but I think I'll hang onto the Flying Club. I think it's time I settled down, too . . ."

He walked her back to the Crosby home. He waited by the gate. The shadows from the old oak screened the starlight, and he saw her face dimly.

"I'll be at the dance Saturday night," he said slowly. "Will you be there?"

She nodded.

He hesitated a moment, wanting to kiss her, but remembering the other incidents between them. He said, "Good night, Carol."

She put her hands on his arms and kissed him, a quick warm pressure of the lips. Then she turned and went quickly up the walk to the door.

He walked back to the main section of town, chewing on an unlighted cigar. He came into River Road, and the night was warm and the stars brighter than he remembered them. Beyond the town the shadowed rangeland, unmarred by ugly oil rigs, ran to the far tumble of hills. The night wind carried the ineffable fragrance of far places.

He muttered, "You're in love, Havolin," and he started to whistle. He turned south on River Road, and when he came abreast of the Palace Bar he turned inside.

He paused just within the swinging doors, his glance searching for Thompson at the bar and among the tables. But the gambler was nowhere in sight. He elbowed up to the bar and waited with his foot on the scarred rail until a mutton-chop-whiskered bartender came over.

"Is Mr. Thompson in?"

The bartender shook his head. "Haven't seen him since noon." He waited, and Brett ordered a drink. He dawdled over it. He felt strangely excited, a little high, although this was his first drink of the day — then he remembered what he had to do Saturday night and some of the anticipation left him.

He pushed his glass away and went over to watch a poker game. A few minutes later one of the players left and he sat in the man's place. The game was for small stakes, played mostly for fun . . . The three men at the table were obviously merchants from their small talk.

Brett was holding his third hand when a tough-looking man with a cast in his left eye came in and pounded on the bar for service. He was an angular slab of a man, mean-looking, with a belt gun showing on his left hip. His voice was rasping and loud enough for everyone to hear.

"Where's Mae?"

The bartender told him Mae wasn't in tonight. He smiled. "Maybe she's entertaining someone else tonight, Mick."

Mick's hand dropped to his gunbutt. "She better not be with someone else!" he snarled. He seemed a little wobbly on his feet, but he poured himself a drink from the bottle the bartender slid to him and drank it in one gulp. "If I find her with someone else I'll kill them both!"

"Better go to bed," the bartender advised, suddenly serious, "before someone tells the sheriff you're packing a gun. You know the town rules."

"To hell with Hogan!" Mick snarled.

A burly man in a flowered waistcoat detached himself from a corner table and went over to Mick. He tapped the man on the shoulder. He was Thompson's bouncer, and he looked quietly capable.

"Finish that drink and get out of here!"

Mick started to argue, then subsided. Grumbling, he tossed silver on the counter and went out, and the thin, nervous man across from Brett said: "Mick's sure gone on that Mae girl. I wouldn't want to be the man she's with tonight — not in the mood he's in right now."

"I wouldn't want to tangle with him myself," Brett agreed. He won the next three hands, lost the last, and decided to quit. He picked up his money, saw he was ahead four dollars and fifty cents. He stopped by the bar, laid the money on the counter.

"Take a bottle over to that table," he said. "My compliments."

He left the Palace Bar and headed for the hotel. He had a day to kill before Saturday, and he knew what he wanted to do. He had never really looked over the Flying Club . . .

He turned once, some vague instinct tugging at him. He saw no one behind him. He shrugged. He didn't expect trouble tonight.

The desk clerk was not in sight when he walked into the lobby. He paused by the settee next to the potted palm and picked up the paper someone had left there. Folding it under his arm, he went around the counter and took his key from the hook under number ten. He was humming softly as he went upstairs.

He heard the lobby door open and close behind him; he was around the middle landing, and he was interested in who had come into the hotel. He was still humming as he paused by his door.

Light seeped under the panels, touching his booted toes. He frowned. He had not left a light burning when he had gone to pick up Carol Armstrong. But it was burning now. Someone was inside his room, waiting . . . His hand reached up to his belt and then he remembered his Colt was stowed away in his saddle bag.

He turned the knob and shoved the door open . . .

A girl was sitting on his bed, cleaning her nails. She was blonde, painted, and dressed in a flimsy nightgown. He had never seen her before.

"Hi, handsome," she greeted him casually. "Come on in."

Brett waited.

"It's just little me," the girl said. She put her straw-colored head to one side and pouted. "I thought you might be lonesome."

Havolin closed the door. He looked around. There was no closet in the room, no place for anyone to hide, unless he hid under the bed. The girl was obviously alone. He couldn't guess how long she had been waiting, but she had made herself at home. Her bag lay on the chair by the bed, and some of her clothes were strewn over the covers.

He remembered he had locked the door when he had left, leaving the key with the clerk. But this girl could very easily have picked up his key, after reading his room number on the register while the clerk was out, opened his door and returned the key to its hook.

He thumbed his hat back on his head, and a hard grin split his lips. He knew a frame when he saw one — but he wondered what was behind this one.

"All right," he said quietly. "I'll help you pack. Be a good girl and don't scream. I'd sure hate to backhand that pretty mouth."

She widened her blue eyes. "Why, Brett!" She had a sort of breathless Southern accent. "You know you asked me to come here and wait for you."

Brett's voice raised in harsh impatience. "You know you're lying! Now get some clothes on while I stuff these —"

He didn't hear the man come to the door. It slammed open and Mick stood framed in it, his gun in his hand. He filled the space, a big, ugly man with the smell of whiskey on him.

"Thought I'd find you here, Mae!" he snarled. "Had to bust Joe in the mouth before he told me. Said you had a new feller — this redheaded runt!"

Mae stood up beside Brett. "Leave us alone, Mick!" Her voice was loud enough to reach down into the lobby. Brett heard doors open cautiously in the hallway.

"The devil I'll leave him alone!" Mick snarled. "I'm gonna break him in two!"

It was an old frame, and Mae dropped all pretense now. She smiled at Mick. "He's all yours," she said, and started to turn away.

Brett caught her by the arm, whirled her around and sent her flying toward the man in the doorway.

Mick's gun went off, and the bullet tore through the plastered wall. The girl screamed in terror. Mick staggered back as she collided with him, and his gun went off again; this bullet splintered through the floor.

Brett piled into both of them, slamming against them with his shoulder. They all spilled out into the hall, and the girl screamed again. Mick tried to scramble up and level his Colt at Brett. Havolin kicked it out of his hand, brought his knee up into Mick's face, then chopped down with a hard twisting right. Mick groaned and fell against the wall and slid down.

134

Brett scooped up the Colt Mick had dropped. He straightened and eyed the men in the doorways. The girl was scrunched against the wall, holding her hands over her bosom. Men were gawking at her.

Steps pounded on the stairs. The clerk appeared around the landing, closely paced by a big, sleepy-eyed man holding a gun. They came into the hallway and stopped a few feet from Mick, who was trying to get up. Blood from his dripping nose splattered the floor.

The clerk spluttered. "Who's that woman? And that shooting — if there are damages —"

"I had company," Brett cut in coldly. "Nobody I invited. I was telling her to pack when this yahoo busted in and started shooting —" He made a quick gesture with the gun. "If there's damages, bill him!"

The clerk gulped. The big man behind him said: "I'll get the sheriff, Tad."

"I'm right behind you," Hogan said. He came down the hallway, a tall man with a scowl on his face. He stopped by Mick and looked at Brett and the girl standing against the wall.

"Still getting into trouble?" he murmured.

"Just a little misunderstanding," Brett said. "This gent put two and two together and tried to make it come out five."

Hogan looked at the girl. "Where's her clothes?"

"In my room," Brett replied. "I was packing for her when this big bad hombre busted in."

"All right!" the sheriff snapped at her. "Get something on!"

The girl sidled past Brett and ducked into the room. Hogan reached down and hauled the bloody-faced Mick to his feet.

He propped him up against the wall, wrinkled his nose at the strong whiskey odor. "You got anything to say before I jail you?"

"He stole my girl!" Mick snarled. There was blood in his mouth and he smeared it across his face as he tried wiping it with the back of his hand.

"I never saw the lady until five minutes ago," Brett denied coldly. "Even a thick-skulled lawman like you can see someone wanted to frame me tonight."

Hogan's eyes narrowed. "Another crack like that and I'll bend that Colt you're holding across your skull, fella."

"He's a liar!" Mick cried. "Joe Larkin kin prove it. He saw the note Mae got from this jasper, offering her a hundred dollars for —"

"All right, cut it!" Hogan snapped. "We don't need the details." He turned to Brett. "Where's the girl?"

Havolin turned and walked into his room. The girl wasn't there. Her bag still lay open on the chair and her clothes were scattered on the bed. By the wash stand the window curtains moved gently. He walked to them and put his head through the open window and looked out on the side gallery and knew Mae was gone.

He walked back to the sheriff. "She took the porch way out," he said curtly.

"Never mind," Hogan muttered. "I know where to find her." He held out his hand. "I'll take that gun, Havolin."

Brett handed it to him. "You can forget this, Sheriff," he said bleakly, "the way you forgot about Tony. But somebody framed me tonight; somebody who wants me killed." He saw a cold smile start in Hogan's eyes, and he went on harshly: "The way it was set up, this jasper could have killed me and maybe gotten away with it. The girl was probably set to swear I forced her in here."

Hogan said thinly: "There you go again, Havolin — doing my job for me. Doing a lot of guessing, mostly."

"You know any other reasons for tonight?" Brett snarled.

"I'll tell you when I find out," Hogan said. He hauled Mick around and shoved him down the hall. "Lock your door tonight, Havolin — she might come back."

His face was deadpan as he said it, and Brett couldn't figure out if he was serious or joking. The sheriff didn't strike him as a joking man.

He stood by the door, watching the sheriff and Mick go down the stairs, followed by the clerk and the big man. The spectators disappeared.

Brett went inside his room, closed the door, and eyed the clothes strewn about his bed with jaundiced eyes. Whoever had killed Tony and tried this way of getting him wasn't going to stop now . . .

CHAPTER
ELEVEN

Havolin didn't see Carol the next morning. He stopped by the sheriff's office and found Ray Hogan going through some papers on his desk.

"I want to see Mick," he said. "I want to ask him a few questions."

"He's not here," Hogan said shortly. He didn't look up from his desk.

Brett said incredulously: "You let him go?"

"This morning."

Brett stood over the desk. "We haven't hit it off from the first day, have we, Sheriff?" he said tightly. "You've gone out of your way to make it tough for me." He put his palms on the desk, and his face was dark with anger. "Someone put that girl and Mick up to framing me! The man who did that probably killed Tony! And you let Mick go!"

Hogan lifted his eyes to Brett. "Mick was jailed for disturbing the peace. I kept him locked up overnight and let him go this morning. If you want to prefer charges, I'll pick him up again."

"You don't believe my story, do you?"

Hogan's pale eyes held an angry glitter. "I checked on Mae last night. She's an entertainer in the Tin Cup

Saloon. She said you paid her for — well, you know what the story is." He lifted up a hand to stop Havolin. "You fool! She'll stick to that story in court. Joe Larkin plays piano in the Tin Cup — he told me he saw the note Mae got from you. Now what do you want me to do?"

Brett stood up. "All right," he said grimly. "Tony got a slug in him and nobody cared — except me. Well, Sheriff, I'm luckier than Tony. I know what I'm bucking. I've got a Colt in my saddle — it's been there from the day you told me no guns were allowed in town. Next time I come to town I'm going to be wearing it, Hogan!"

He turned and slammed the door behind him. Hogan settled back against his chair, took a deep breath. The strain was beginning to show in his face . . .

Brett rode back to the Flying Club. He wanted to go over the terrain, see what Consolidated's scout might have found. Brett had wildcatted a couple of dusters with Sam Morrison and he had learned something about oil formations.

He arrived at the ranch about noon, ate a meager meal, and rode out again. He rode most of the afternoon in a wide looping swing that took him from the Creosote Cliffs to the Big Wash. Once he stopped and studied the oily film on water oozing out of a crack in a hill.

He was satisfied now. Even Tony might have seen it, he thought, if Tony had been looking for it. But Tony had come seven hundred miles from Beaumont and had had no reason to believe he was any closer to oil than that. A man finds what he looks for, and Tony had come to this valley looking for farmland, not oil.

He turned the steeldust back toward the Flying Club. He was going to have a busy day tomorrow, he thought. He'd find Mick, if he was still in town — there were ways of getting a man to talk.

He remembered that Hogan had said that the girl in his room last night was an entertainer at the Tin Cup. A new possibility made him scowl. The Tin Cup Saloon was the favorite hangout of Big Diamond riders. This was understandable, in view of the enmity between Jack Thompson, who owned the Palace Bar, and Bully Armstrong.

Armstrong may have put Mick and Mae up to what happened last night. If he had come to town and seen him with Carol . . . ? It was a new angle, but Havolin couldn't dismiss it. Armstrong had proved he was capable of a thing like that when he had sent Prel after his daughter . . .

He came back to the Flying Club at sundown. The two windows facing west seemed on fire, reflecting the great blaze over the low hills . . . The big pepper tree had an unreal look, doused in the fading red rays.

The steeldust suddenly snorted warningly and began to mince slowly, as though it smelled danger.

Brett roused. "What's the matter, boy? Something scare you?"

The horse tossed his head. He whinnied softly. From somewhere behind the shed an animal answered with an eager whicker.

140

Brett went tense. He searched the quiet scene. He saw nothing move, but he remained alert.

He touched the steeldust with his heels, and the animal moved slowly off to the house . . .

It was the rooster that started it. It came out of the barn in a squawking, protesting bundle of feathers. Brett jerked the steeldust around in time to see the tall figure of Mick step out, a rifle in his hands.

He jerked the steeldust around and dug in his heels, and the rifle shot spanked the stillness. The animal shuddered. It never completed the turn. It fell on its side, and Brett barely rolled free. He lay half stunned, and the echoes of the shot rolled back from the distant hills.

The silence gathered again. He heard another man's hard voice say, "Let's make sure of him, Mick. Put a couple more slugs in him!"

Brett's fingers sought the Colt butt pressing hard against his stomach. He gathered himself for one desperate scramble.

Another voice intruded now, flat and grimly final. "Got here a mite too late, Mick, but in time to see you both hang!"

There was a snarling curse and a shot, and then two quick successive reports. Brett was on his feet, his Colt in his hand. He saw Mick break for the shed, whirl, and pump a quick shot at him. His own Colt bucked in his palm.

He saw dust fly from Mick's wool shirt. The man turned as though to walk away. He took a stumbling half-step and fell.

In front of the open cabin door another man lay, sprawled face down. The tall figure of the sheriff was standing over him — the Colt in Hogan's fist was still smoking.

The lawman turned and looked at Brett, and his voice was flat. "You've got more lives than a cat, Havolin."

Brett looked down at the steeldust which had taken Mick's bullet. He stepped over the dead animal and walked toward Hogan.

"Reckon I owe you my life," he said, but there was little thanks in his voice.

The sheriff holstered his gun and took the makings from his shirt pocket. "You don't owe me anything," he said flatly. "I let Mick out hoping he'd lead me to whoever hired him. Instead he and Rod Harris left town together. I followed them." He shrugged. "They weren't expecting anyone to trail them, so I didn't have much trouble. Looks like they came to smoke you out, and when they didn't find you home, they decided to wait for you."

"Thanks, anyway," Brett said dryly. He waved toward the house. "If you'll hang around a while, I'll have coffee on the fire." He grinned insolently. "Cow-country hospitality, Sheriff."

Hogan shook his head. "Some other time, mebbe . . ."

Brett made a gesture toward the body at the sheriff's feet. "Who's he? Who's he work for?"

"Harris? He and Mick don't work. Not steady, anyway. They rode for Big Diamond just long enough

142

to draw a month's pay, came into town and said they quit. I heard Armstrong caught them mavericking some of his beef and almost hung them before his son stopped it. But Armstrong never came to the law with it, and you can take your pick as to what really happened."

Big Diamond again, Brett thought coldly.

"They've got horses behind the shed, Havolin. I'll get mine from that clump of trees where I hid it —"

He joined Brett a few minutes later. The mounts Harris and Mick had ridden had evidently been hired from the Benton Wells livery.

Brett said: "Leave the gray, Sheriff. I don't seem to have luck with horses. And I'll want to ride into town tomorrow." His grin was as cold as winter ice. "I won't want to miss the Big Diamond shindig for the world."

Ray Hogan looked down on him. He nodded slowly. "Reckon you won't, Havolin. Just remember, I'll be there, too!"

He swung away, leading the other animal with the two bodies draped across the saddle. He rode tall, a hard and unfathomable man, toward the distant, darkening road.

CHAPTER
TWELVE

Brett awakened early Saturday morning. But he took his time shaving and dressing. He tidied up the place, filled the wood box. He brought water for the gray in the shed, broke open a bag of grain and tossed some to the cocky rooster who had evaded the prowling coyote for another night.

It was almost noon when he saddled the gray and rode to the Marlin ranch.

Mady Marlin came to the door before he dismounted. She stood small and frail in the doorway, her eyes blinking at him from behind her spectacles. She was wearing a crisply starched black dress and her white hair was pinned in a neat bun on her neck. She lifted up a thin, translucent hand to shade her eyes from the sun.

"Why, Mister Havolin! Please come in. I've just made tea — do you like tea — ?"

"I was weaned on black coffee," Brett interrupted gently. He looked toward the open-faced shed where he had noticed the red-wheeled buggy on his first visit here. It was gone.

"I came by to see Lorna," he said. "I have good news for her."

"Oh!" Mrs. Marlin looked up at him, her eyes behind the glasses alert as a bird's. "You have decided to sell, Mr. Havolin?"

"No."

Mady Marlin smiled somewhat uncertainly. "Lorna's gone to the dance in Benton Wells. Mr. Baggett — of the bank, you know — came for her." She added a little apologetically, "You know how young people are? I was like that myself, at her age. But I married early. Too early. A man who had no money —" Her eyes seemed dark and withdrawn now, as though she had slipped back into those bitter years. "I would never allow Lorna to be so foolish, Mister Havolin."

Brett shrugged. "I'm sure you wouldn't," he said softly. "But of course you won't have to worry about money any more."

Mrs. Marlin blinked. "What are you saying?"

"Hasn't Mr. Baggett told you and Lorna about the oil?"

Mady Marlin's voice was almost a whisper. "I don't know what you're talking about, Mister Havolin."

Brett leaned forward in saddle, his tone confidential. "Oil, Mrs. Marlin. There's been an oil scout for Consolidated making a survey. It looks like the Flying Club and this place have become valuable property. If Consolidated is interested, they'll pay plenty for a lease." Brett smiled. "They may even want to buy your place, Mrs. Marlin. But I wouldn't sell. I'd hold out for a lease and oil royalties instead —"

"You say Walter Baggett knew about this?" the Marlin woman asked. Her voice was strained. "Walter's known about the oil survey?"

Brett nodded. "He must have known it several months ago." He frowned. "No wonder Mr. Baggett wanted to buy the Flying Club. He knew how much it really was worth."

Mrs. Marlin hardly seemed elated at the news. She said uncertainly: "I'm sure Lorna will be surprised when she hears about this —"

Havolin settled back in saddle. "Well — good day, Mrs. Marlin. I expect to see Lorna at the dance tonight. I'll tell her myself."

He turned away from the small yard. When he was across the creek he looked back. Mrs. Marlin was still in the doorway, a small, frail figure in the reddening rays of the sun . . .

The courthouse assembly room, by day a scene of dignified emptiness, came to life every Saturday night. It was customary for the weekly dance to be held there, where the young folk could get in some courting, the older ones a bit of gallivanting, and where the gossip of the week made the rounds of the benches where the older women were content to sit and keep a watchful eye on their daughters.

But this Saturday night was special. This was the night of the Big Diamond shindig. This was the night when the celebration was on Bully Armstrong. Every saloon in town was holding open house with the understanding that the night's bill would be paid for by Big Diamond.

The gigs, buggies and wagons were lined up on either side of the quiet, oak-shadowed street as far back as River Road when Brett rode into town. He came in on a deserted main street, and he heard the sounds of laughter and wailing fiddles long before he turned the gray toward the courthouse.

He found Lawyer Kinsman in the Dusty Hole, slumped over a table. The celebration must have started early for the attorney.

"Yeah — yeah," he mumbled as Brett shook him. He focused bloodshot eyes on Brett's face. "Sure — I told them. They laughed at you, Havolin! You're crazy! Fifty thousand dollars —"

Brett turned away. He had not expected any takers; all he wanted to know was that they had been informed.

He'd start with Bully Armstrong tonight.

He rode toward the sound of merriment until he found a small break in the parked vehicles and left his horse there, tethered to a pole support.

The street ended in a wide square with the white clapboard courthouse facing it. A big tree shadowed the entrance, from which came the contagious sounds of celebration.

Havolin started down the shadowed walk. He was less than twenty feet away when Sheriff Hogan's voice stopped him.

"This is Big Diamond's night, Havolin." Hogan's face was in shadow, but his voice was clear. "You come to celebrate?"

Havolin shrugged. He could barely make out the sheriff under the big oak. The lawman was wearing a gun. Brett remembered that he was wearing his, too.

"I've come to celebrate," he replied coldly.

Hogan was silent a moment. "You'll find a coat closet to the left of the door when you go in," he said finally. "Old Tod will take your hat — and your gun!"

"Fair enough," Brett said. He walked past the sheriff and up the three steps to the courthouse. The door was open, and a little light came through. He hesitated in the hallway. At the far end double walnut doors were folded back, giving him a view of the big assembly room. Bright streamers decorated the big room, extended in swirls of color into the hallway. Several men, stiff in their Sunday suits, were clustered about the entrance.

Brett turned to the door, where an old, watery-eyed man took his hat and his gunbelt. "Plumb crowded tonight, stranger," he squeaked. He hefted the gunbelt and frowned disapprovingly. "Most folks hereabouts have quit wearing these to town. Ain't been a gunfight in Benton Wells for more than three — nope, four years." He turned to search among the crowded hooks for a place to hang Havolin's hat and belt. "They'll be right here, near the door. Easy to pick up when you —"

"Why, hello, Havolin!"

Brett turned to face Walter Baggett and Lorna, who had come up to the door. Baggett was slickly groomed, poised, sure of himself. Lorna hung on his arm. She had on a pale blue dress which set off her mass of golden hair. Her eyes met Brett's in cool, amused appraisal.

Baggett was saying affably, "Glad you decided to come — good Lord!" he ejaculated. "What happened to your face?"

"Cut it shaving," Brett answered shortly.

The banker's eyes held an amused glint. "Well, see you inside. Lorna found it a bit stuffy — we're stepping out for a few minutes."

"Just a minute," Havolin said. "Are you still interested?"

"In what?" Baggett's voice held a thin puzzlement.

"In the Flying Club. I asked Kinsman to tell you my price."

"Oh!" Baggett laughed. "I can't believe you're serious, Mr. Havolin. Fifty thousand dollars!" He took Lorna's arm. "See you inside later, Havolin."

Brett watched them go out. Lorna's laughter rippled softly in the night. He took a deep breath.

How many men had Lorna Marlin had on the string? Tony. The sheriff. Walter Baggett. What did Lorna Marlin really want? Tony was dead now. But he must have been encouraged once. More than encouraged, Brett suspected — or Tony would not have written to him about marriage.

Where did Ray Hogan fit in? Was it because Lorna Marlin liked the way she could twist him around her fingers — liked to tease him?

Walter Baggett he could understand. Baggett could give her position, money — all the things Mady Marlin wanted for her daughter.

What had Lorna wanted of him? The Flying Club? But unless her mother had been lying, Lorna didn't know about the oil survey. Then why had she wanted it? Unless it was the banker's money that was behind her

— unless it had been Baggett's indirect way of attempting to get the ranch on Piute Creek.

Brett turned his thoughts to the dance. He hadn't lied when he told Hogan he had come for the celebration. A private celebration, he thought grimly — strictly between Bully Armstrong and himself.

He paused at the entrance to the dance floor, his glance moving among the dancing couples. He glimpsed Carol Armstrong, looking cool in a white dress. She was dancing with a tall, gangly farm boy who was moving stiffly around the floor. Havolin's survey took in the crowded benches. He didn't see Thompson among the men against the side wall, which didn't surprise him. Nor did he see Chet Armstrong.

But most of Benton Wells was here, he judged. And the cynical thought came to him that though people seemed to dislike the Armstrongs, they didn't mind drinking Bully Armstrong's liquor.

He spotted the Big Diamond boss finally, standing by the table with the big glass punchbowl. The punch was obviously intended for the ladies, for they were the only ones who seemed to partake of it.

Havolin started to make his way along the edge of the floor toward Armstrong. He stepped carefully, avoiding the feet of the women on the benches. Two boys, young enough to be home in bed, came charging toward him. Havolin evaded them. He was in a partially cleared section of the big room when he heard Carol's voice.

"Brett!"

150

He turned and faced the floor. Carol was coming toward him — her partner was standing awkwardly by, being nudged by other dancers. He looked at Brett with unfriendly eyes.

Carol searched his face. "I'd been expecting you earlier —"

He smiled. "Save me the next dance?"

She nodded, but her voice was apprehensive. "Where are you going?"

"To have a few words with your father," he said quietly.

"No!" Carol's voice caused heads to turn, brought the gangly boy eagerly to her side.

"He bothering you, Miss Carol?"

Brett walked away from her. She stood looking after him, ignoring her partner's question . . .

Havolin was within ten feet of the Big Diamond boss when Armstrong noticed him. The rancher was listening to a buxom woman chattering in his ear. He glanced up to see Havolin coming toward him, and for a brief instant his eyes mirrored sharp disbelief. Then a grudging smile crinkled his lips.

Two Big Diamond hands saw Brett at the same time and moved up to take their place beside Armstrong.

Brett said levelly: "I wasn't in good form the other night, Armstrong. I've come to give you another chance."

Armstrong glanced at the door behind him. "There's an alley out there, son. You want to keep this private?"

Brett nodded.

The big rancher shrugged. He turned to the tall, straw-haired man at his left. "Keep the fiddlers playing, Blake. And don't let anyone follow us. I'll be back in three minutes."

The Big Diamond hands stepped sullenly aside, letting Brett through. Havolin followed Armstrong through the side door into the coolness of the alley.

He closed the door behind him and leaned against it, letting his eyes accustom themselves to the dim light of the stars and a high riding sliver of moon.

Armstrong had moved into the alley and was shedding his coat. His voice was short. "Let's get this over with, Havolin."

Brett stepped away from the door. "You've had a real licking coming to you for twenty years," he said grimly. "Too bad someone didn't kick your teeth in before you got too big for your hat. It would have saved your son and your daughter a lot of grief."

Armstrong balled his big hands. "Let's quit the big talk, son," he growled. "I'm in a hurry —"

Havolin hit him. His right fist smeared Armstrong's mouth with blood, straightened him. Brett's left whipped around as Armstrong gagged. He felt the shock of impact clear to his shoulder.

Armstrong's head twisted around under the blow. He brought up his hands to cover his face from the blows he couldn't evade, could barely see. He stumbled forward, spitting blood, an incredulous snarl twisting his battered lips.

Brett's right hand sank three inches into Armstrong's unflexed stomach. The rancher's breath whooshed out.

152

He stood stricken, his bloody mouth gaping, trying to suck in air.

Brett stepped in and contemptuously back-handed him across the face.

Bully Armstrong was already sagging when the backhand reached him. He fell sideways, hitting the dirt with a hard impact.

Brett stood over him, breathing easily. He had learned in a rough school that the man who struck the first blow usually gained an advantage that was hard to overcome. He waited now, feeling little pity for this big man pawing the ground at his feet.

Armstrong came to his feet. He brought the back of his hand across his bloody mouth. His eyes had a glazed, uncertain look.

"Before we finish this thing, Armstrong," Brett said bleakly, "I want to know one thing. When did you find out there was oil on the Flying Club?"

Bully Armstrong's head came up, and Brett saw the naked surprise in the rancher's eyes. "Oil?" Armstrong dragged in a deep breath. "What are you talking about?"

"The oil scout from Consolidated!" Brett snapped. "Don't tell me you didn't know. He was up here, making a survey, just before Tony was killed —"

The alley exploded behind Brett. A red flash momentarily lighted the night, and in that brief lurid glare Havolin saw the shock in Armstrong's face. He knew Armstrong had been shot before the big man started to crumble.

His own surprise held him inactive for an instant longer. A hard object skittered along the ground and banged against his foot. Havolin turned, and the glint of the object caught his eye. He lunged for it, scooping the gun up, and recognition followed the familiar feel of the walnut butt in his palm. It was his own Colt he was holding! And the import of this suddenly panicked him.

The music had stopped as though the shot had switched it off. He heard voices raised in questioning shouts, heard the pounding of feet toward the side door. Even before they reached it Havolin knew what those angry men would think, what Sheriff Hogan would think. The lawman was only waiting for a thing like this to hang him!

Havolin turned and ran.

Carol Armstrong knelt beside her father. Armstrong was trying to sit up. The effort strained his neck muscles, distorted his bloody features. His shirt front was a dark, sticky mess.

Carol's voice was broken with grief. "He told me he wanted to talk to you. I didn't dream he'd —"

The old cattleman's jaw bulged. "Young red-headed fool — he didn't shoot me. Shot came from behind — up the alley —"

Sheriff Hogan pushed through the murmuring crowd and stood over Carol. He snapped an order: "One of you men get the doc. Pronto!" He hunkered down by the girl. His voice was brusque. "Who shot you, Frank?"

Armstrong licked his lips. "Don't know. But it wasn't Havolin." He wagged his head slowly. "Darned fool thought I killed Tony. Said something about an oil scout from Consolidated finding oil on the Flying Club. Seemed to be sure I killed his friend —"

He clenched his teeth against a sharp stab of pain.

Carol said sharply: "Where's the doctor! Someone please help me with him. We've got to get him inside."

Sheriff Hogan moved away as the doctor came hurrying up the alleyway. He heard the medico say quickly: "Bring him to my office. I can't work here."

Hogan didn't hurry. He walked out of the alley into the square in front of the courthouse. He stood under the big oak and reached in his pocket for a cigar. He didn't light it. He thought of Havolin, and a grudging smile touched his mouth.

He walked up the street, a tall and deliberate man, knowing what he had to do and not liking it. He stopped in at the corner bar and had a drink. The bartender was curious about the shot he had heard — but the look on Hogan's face discouraged his questions.

The sheriff walked out. He turned in at the stable where he kept his horse and saddled up. He took his time. When he rode out of Benton Wells, he headed west, for the Marlin place . . .

CHAPTER
THIRTEEN

The moon came out from behind a cloud and lightened the gloom in the small yard. Wind ruffled a puff of dust toward the open shed where Brett Havolin waited.

He had been waiting twelve minutes, but it seemed a lot longer. He hunkered on his heels, his gun thrust in his waistband.

A lamp, turned low, cast its wan light against the windows of the Marlin house. He wondered briefly if Mady Marlin was awake, waiting for the return of her daughter.

The Marlin cow moved restlessly in its stall on the other side of the partition. The night was soft with late summer heat. The insect chorus made a quiet melody in the darkness.

Havolin had gone over all the angles before riding here. He was still surprised at how easily he had circled, slipped back down the darkened street and reached his horse; at the lack of pursuit.

But he knew one thing. Walter Baggett and Lorna Marlin would be showing up soon. And Baggett had to be his man! By the simple process of elimination, it had to be Baggett who had killed Tony, and who tonight had tried to frame him by killing Armstrong!

He heard the buggy on the road before it splashed across the shallow water at the fording. A board creaked in the house, and Brett frowned. Was Mrs. Marlin still up?

The buggy wheeled into the yard, and in the dim moonlight Brett saw that Walter Baggett was driving. The banker pulled up by the door. Lorna Marlin hesitated.

"Do you think they've caught him yet?" Her voice sounded worried.

Walter patted her bare arm. "That's not for us to worry about. We'll let Hogan do it for us."

"Ray's getting suspicious," Lorna said. "I can't deal with him much longer. If only he would —"

"Do what?" Brett asked coldly. "Hang me?"

He came away from the darkness of the shed, into the light of the Marlin yard. "Is that what's worrying you, Lorna?"

The girl shivered. Baggett was still holding the reins. He ran his tongue over his lips.

"Gave us quite a start, Havolin," he said shakily. "We heard you had killed Frank Armstrong. Can't say that I blame you — after what he did to you."

"I didn't kill Armstrong," Brett said.

The banker made a small motion with his shoulder. "Lorna and I heard a shot. I tried to get close. But there was a great confusion around someone in the alley behind the courthouse. I heard someone say, 'Havolin shot Armstrong!'" Baggett tried a weak smile. "I thought I'd better take Lorna home then."

The door opened, creaking softly. Mady Marlin stood in the dim wash of lamplight. She was still wearing her black dress and her spectacles. But she didn't look frail and small at this moment — not the way she was holding the Sharps rifle.

Lorna gave a gasp of surprise. "Mother! I thought you'd be in bed!"

"I've been waiting for you," Mrs. Marlin said. "Waiting for you and Mr. Baggett."

Lorna's words tumbled out. "There was trouble — at the dance. Walter decided to take me home —"

"I've been waiting," Mrs. Marlin continued, cutting through her daughter's explanation as though she didn't hear it. Her voice sounded indistinct, as though it came from a distance. She was looking up at Baggett, whatever emotion was in her eyes shielded by her spectacles. "Why didn't you tell me, Walter?"

The banker glanced at Brett, standing silent and watchful, waiting. His tone was sharp. "Tell you what, Mrs. Marlin?"

"About the oil."

Baggett started. "Oil?" His laughter was too quick. "What oil?"

"The oil on our property. Mine and Mr. Havolin's. The oil Consolidated is interested in."

Baggett looked down at Havolin. "What are you up to?" he shouted. "What have you been telling this crazy woman?"

Lorna grabbed his arm, pulling him around. Her voice was fierce. "Is it true, Walter?"

Brett's voice answered for Baggett. "It's true, Lorna. He's known about the oil survey for two months, since before Tony Mareno was killed."

Lorna's fingers dug into the tight-mouthed banker's arm. "Is that why you had me play up to Havolin?" she breathed. "So that he would sell to me? Was that behind the agreement by which I was to turn the Flying Club over to you?"

He didn't say anything, and her eyes widened. "That's what you wanted, isn't it? That's why you wanted to buy our place, too. And I was willing to go along with you. Because you told me you would marry me —"

Baggett shoved her away. She tumbled over the side of the seat, clinging desperately. He kicked at her, his lips twisting hard against his bared teeth. Lorna screamed and tried to hold on as the startled team lunged against their collars.

Brett ran forward, sliding his Colt under his belt. Lorna was falling. He twisted to catch her, and her weight staggered him. Over her shoulder he saw Baggett slap the team with the loose end of the reins.

The Sharps made a heavy explosion in the night. Baggett fell backward over the seat, as though he had been kicked in the face. The buggy lurched as the frightened animals broke into a run. Baggett's body tumbled over the side and lay crumpled in the moonlight.

Havolin set Lorna Marlin on her feet. He walked slowly to the slight woman slumped against the door. A rider was coming into the yard at a run. But Havolin didn't turn around until he had taken the Sharps rifle from Mrs. Marlin.

Sheriff Hogan pulled up by Baggett's body, glanced down at the dead man before directing his attention to Brett.

Mady Marlin was mumbling: "Always wanted everything for Lorna. Things I never had. That's why I killed Tony. He was a nice boy. But he had nothing. I didn't want to see Lorna forced to live a life that would finally kill her —"

Hogan climbed down from his saddle. "I thought Lorna had killed Tony," he said. His voice sounded very tired. "Tony was killed by a heavy caliber bullet. A Sharps 50/60." He looked at Brett, explaining, "There's only one gun like that in the valley. I thought it was Lorna who killed him. I didn't know why. I didn't want to find out why."

Havolin shrugged. Lorna Marlin was crying softly, her shoulders slumped. "About tonight," Brett began, "I didn't kill Armstrong —"

"He isn't dead!" Hogan muttered. "He cleared you. Called you a redheaded, stubborn fool — but he said you didn't shoot him!"

Lorna's face turned to the sheriff, white in the moonlight. "Walter shot Frank Armstrong," she said. "He had me talk to Tod while he took Brett's gun. We had seen where Tod hung it. I didn't really know what he was up to. He took the gun and went outside and down the alley. He thought he had killed Armstrong. He wanted to have the killing blamed on Brett —"

Hogan walked up to her. "It's all right," he said. His voice was low, expectant.

Havolin shrugged. "You want me now, Sheriff?"

The lawman didn't even look at him. "No."

Brett turned away. He started to walk toward the shadows behind the shed where he had left the gray.

Mady Marlin's mumbling stirred the silence behind him. "Killed Tony because he had nothing. And all the time there was oil here, enough oil to make us rich —"

Brett looked back once. Lorna's face was buried in Hogan's shirt front. The sheriff was standing tall, his hand smoothing her golden hair.

Brett smiled coldly. He didn't envy the lawman his problems.

It was noon, a week later, when Brett rode into the yard of the Flying Club. He had sent Morrison a wire that he was not joining him in Beaumont, and he had looked up the sheriff at his request.

"Mae broke down about that affair in the hotel," Hogan told Brett. "Walter Baggett hired them for the job. When it fell through Mick talked his partner Harris into joining him to kill you. Baggett had promised Mick a thousand dollars if they got rid of you."

"I thought for a time that Frank Armstrong might have hired them," he said. "I'm glad he didn't."

"Frank's a mean old cuss," Hogan said. There was no real friendliness in his voice; he would never like Havolin. But there was respect between them. "But he ain't the kind to hire others to kill a man he hates."

Brett shrugged.

"I hear you're staying on at the Flying Club," Hogan said.

"I'll try my hand at it," Havolin admitted.

Hogan smiled briefly. He reached in a drawer and took out a box of cigars. He pushed them toward the redhead. "They're yours. You've earned them."

Brett took the box with him. He stopped in at the Palace Bar before riding back to the Flying Club.

Thompson was at the table where he had first met him. He looked up as Brett approached. He seemed wary, and older.

"I've got to get one thing straight," Brett said seriously. "If I didn't it would bother me the rest of my life."

Thompson shrugged. He flipped a card face up, and it was a jack of spades. He placed it carefully under a red queen.

"Did you know about the oil survey?"

Thompson didn't look up. "No," he said flatly.

"That story you told me, about why you hated Armstrong —"

"I still hate him." Thompson's eyes met his now, cold and unfriendly. "I had my reasons for telling you." He laughed somewhat bitterly. "The truth wouldn't have sounded so good. I wanted you to hate Armstrong, too."

Brett nodded. "It almost worked out that way," he murmured. "Thanks, anyway —"

He felt better when he rode back to the Flying Club. He saw the roan in the shade of the pepper tree, and when he rode up he smelled bacon frying. He dismounted and walked to the door, holding his eagerness in check.

Carol Armstrong turned from the stove at his step. She wore old range clothes, and there was a smudge of wood ash on her cheek. Her eyes were bright. But she looked at him with a dubious smile, as though not quite sure yet of her reception.

"Hello," she said.

Brett grinned. "Hello yourself."

"Just wanted to be neighborly," Carol volunteered. "Dad's out of bed now and in a chair. He really doesn't need me around any more. Now that he's better he is more like his old self — hard to live with. He and Chet sit on the veranda and growl at each other —"

Brett started toward her. "About time you showed up," he said. "I was getting tired of eating out of cans."

Carol's smile was tremulous. "I hope you don't think —"

She didn't finish. Brett's arms went around her, and she turned her face up to him, all her doubts and anxiety leaving her. "Oh, Brett!" she said softly. "Brett —"